T0043816

# OUR DISTANCE BECAME WATER

# ANDREAS PHILIPPOPOULOS-MIHALOPOULOS
## OUR DISTANCE BECAME WATER

ERIS

London • New York

# contents

**Part I**

*Where We Are Different*

## one

This is what's left of our city. A manic precarity jutting out of a liquid smoothness, desperately trying to stay up, erect, glimmering. But the glow of glass and metal has been overshadowed by the flatness of the waters, already invading the second floors of most large buildings. The old imperial dream, that concentration of colonial sighs and capitalist saliva, is slowly sinking. Its foundations have now been replaced by aquatic life, unexplained sudden gurgles, steady corrosion, liquidity.

The first to go were the deep basements, two and three levels below the ground-floors of the large mansions in the smart areas of the city. Private cinemas and gyms started flooding from within, the water surging from underfloor heating outlets and those hatches that neatly conceal laptop plugs. Next were the swimming pool levels, those penumbras of filtered natural light and mood illuminations, neither quite basement nor ground floor. The pool waters started rising as if emboldened, their fastidious cleanliness mixed with that ubiquitous green shade by now affecting the colours of the whole city. Not just green of course. Tongues of oily blackness, multi-coloured ribbons of assaulting perseverance, clouds of unearthly brownness: the underground tunnels were being washed out; soot and dirt amassed over centuries of digging and hiding were now moving up and mixing with the wetness of pools and humidors.

Bloated sewers made life unbearable during those first months. The muck and the stench were bad enough, but what was truly intolerable was the way this urban belching haunted everyone's dreams, from the youngest to the oldest. Blobby monsters that trembled like oil spills; vessels of things past, done and dusted one would think; ostracised excreta pulsing with memories, guilt, missed opportunities: all these wounds on the fabric of our self-possession bloomed wildly during the first few months.

After the basements, it was just a short gulp before public fountains, paddling lakes, and navigable canals started rising, initially playfully—an open invitation to children and overworked adults to dip in toes and fingers and indulge for a moment in the positives of this soaring chaos. The very first act of the local government, initially rendered helpless by that wave of anxiety that paralysed all structures, was to try and switch off the fountains when they saw that the water spurting out of them had turned sea-weed green, thick with bacteria and other forms of undesired life. But it didn't work—the gurgling force coming from below was impossible to contain. And anyway, it was only a matter of time until all these were also covered by that flat stillness whose only motion was an imperceptible but voracious upwards.

# two

*A few years before the waters.*

That was a time when time meant different things. A time when we could specify appointments with what we now realise was an unfounded, even arrogant, certainty. And so, we specified. The place: the lobby café of a rather grand art-deco hotel—not too busy but not empty either, plenty of available tables in case of error or hesitation. The time: late afternoon, both of us pretending to be busy on our phones, easy walls that suck you in, blurring the line between social defence and monomania.

It had been a very wet week and the café was breathing in the humidity coming from hunched bodies, muddy shoes, and dripping umbrellas rushed into the dry. Our discussion was flowing, although not very smoothly. Yes, we had things in common and we could have talked about them. We might even have done so; neither of us remembers. We mostly talked in question marks, a breathless ping-pong of hooks and dots, neither of us really caring for the replies, or certainly not registering them. We produced the right sounds, of course, but only as growling preludes to the next question. A barrage of forgettable questions and even more forgettable answers in order to conceal the one thing that we knew our skins could not conceal: a sudden desire, a thirst for the other's body and touch and smell that was bubbling inside us. I experienced my desire for you as a river, rough and foamy and yet at the same time darkly ponderous, over which I had to—simply had to— throw all those question marks in order to bridge us on the basis of something less embarrassing, less exposing than that elemental force. Language would do. It usually does. But we failed, despite our best conscious efforts. Every question we threw at each other was aiming not for an answer but for that brief space of rupture between the hook and dot of the question mark. In that echoing space that language forgets, our connection blossomed and our skins carried on communicating, devoid of all social niceties.

My wild gesticulating managed to upset a glass of sparkling water situated too close to me. What you did then was, I now know, the determining gesture of our future: without thinking, without even halting in your effort to answer my no doubt uninteresting question, you dipped your thumb into that agitated body of water and carbon dioxide and started making little waves across the table surface, methodically from left to right. Our fingers were already used to that wave-making movement. We practised it every day with a concentration that belied the casualness of the whole thing. We were both constantly logged in, dwelling in that short space between waves on our respective screens, your face brooding and enigmatic, mine in desperately aloof profile, both of us screaming "please find me". The waves around us stopped when our fingers encountered each other's profile photos. Some sea separated, some rain stood still in mid-air, and the inconsequential act of momentarily reversing the direction of our swiping marked us for each other.

Well, actually no, nothing as earth-shattering as all that. It was just regular online dating, after all. We saw, we swiped, we met. But allow me to carry on thinking that something a little special happened at our first meeting: that the fractal randomness with which our fingers reached out, almost piercing each other's screens, had something decisive to do with the way we have since introduced the water between us—an accidental space where to this day our bodies carry on asserting our desire for each other.

We now know that we had invited the water into our relationship much earlier than the flooding came, long before the augured extinction that was later to engulf our lives. Our love for each other predates our city's unwilling marriage to the water. And our love (and fear and anger and embarrassment and panic and resignation) for water predates everything that was to happen to our city that year.

We used to think of the times of our first love, and, even later, of our love maturing through difficulties, as times where water hardly had a role. As dry times. Except that now, after the rise of the waters, after the establishment of the city's new-found liquid wisdom, we understand something we could not then: that there have never been dry times. We have always been trying to float on the water that we ourselves were obsessively inviting—a perfidious guest that converted us, its eager hosts, into numb hostages.

## waterspeak

I know you well. I am both inside and outside,
crossing your skin, unstoppable.

I am gentle with your bodies, aren't I? See how
I provide for your needs. You would think I am
here for you. I take the shape of your outline, fill
your world with wombs. I become your home, your
dreams, your phobias.

I conduct you, heat and cold, I am your angel, aren't
I? Furious fleet flitting around, reaching where
your little skin-contained identities cannot.

What a dear I am.

Really though, all this is so tiresome. Because,
mark: I have no access to your subconscious. I do
not profess to speak your inner truth.

Sod that, I cannot stand the truth.

I am only carrying your vibrations in my globules
and plopping them up against the other shore.

Oh, and I reflect.
I do this pretty well.

But you are fooled. You seem to forget that I'm not
here for you. I'm here and that's all.

And only for a little while.

In a few battings of the cosmic eyelids, I will be
gone from earth, evaporated in trellises of inter-
planetary frivolity, off to play somewhere else with
things neither better nor worse than you.

So let me put it this way: your anthropomorphising me, your hating me or adoring me, your judging me as too cold, too hot, too dirty, too shallow, too smelly—all this is cute but frankly irrelevant.

You are all an unintended consequence of my being here.

## three

*A few years before the waters.*

By the time the water reached the second floors of the larger buildings, most shops and businesses that could afford to do so had already moved further up. There was a great deal of requisitioning during those times, with the local government desperately trying to find dry spaces for its offices, and in the process its officials being lobbied or even bribed by the better-connected business owners to procure new spaces. This added to the masses of displaced people trying to find accommodation in the taller edifices of the city centre, after their houses and low apartment buildings had been flooded. State controls and the usual civil society guarantees were slowly being eroded, allowing instead a state of permanent exception to settle in.

Still, the city managed to avoid the panic and despair that threatened to invade every single activity, and quickly reinvented itself. There was an ever-expanding programme of initiatives by residents and the government trying to get everyone in the mood for co-operation and creative engagement with this new reality and especially with the refugees from the peripheries; some serious attempts at a working network of municipal boats that connected the main points in the city; a small but adaptable fleet of private boats that operated as taxis and mini buses; a wave of public art projects that took to the waters for inspiration; and a flurry of innovative entrepreneurial activity and productive downsizing on the part of mixed-use shops that had moved from the ground floor up and were trying to lure the residents out of their watery isolation.

Third and fourth floors across the city were quickly becoming the old high streets. Existing corridors linking abandoned flats were being pierced with makeshift shop windows, hastily covered up with sturdy sliding doors at night. An odd thing: these doors were almost never made of glass. Glass sales suffered greatly during these months of endless relocation. Partly no doubt because of the glass's fragility and the difficulty of transporting it. Partly because it was hard to find glass readily available. But partly also because it would seem that none of us wished for yet another reflective surface in addition to the water below. We needed spaces where we would be sheltered from this incessant mirroring. We were becoming blinded by this constant opportunity for self-reflection, this aggressive reminder of our facial expressions, our tastes and clothing, our hairdo errors. We had all developed sophisticated defence mechanisms to hide our creeping fear of the future and our deep-seated anxiety about how we were to carry on providing for ourselves and our loved ones when everything was collapsing around us. So we were trying to avoid looking at ourselves. We would stare even more obsessively at our phones (if electricity provision allowed us to charge them) when waiting for public transport to arrive; we would keep looking up towards the buildings with their constantly changing uses when being driven around on a boat; we would try at any cost to avoid catching our reflection on the water for fear of thinking things we had been waving aside since the rising of the waters. A moment of denial perhaps, but a much needed one.

What we would never tire of, however, provided that we could do it from a safe distance that left any self-reflection out of the picture, was admiring the new watery aesthetics. The usual street-level dirt had been swamped by this flat, homogeneous surface. Even the floating rubbish islands looked photogenic. The waters were broken only by treetops rising up like floating bushes, or by the top part of street lamps, most of them miraculously still working, casting their light deep into the waters around them and for a moment creating the impression that life on the ground was carrying on as before, just a little more refracted, just a little more trembling.

A new sense of pride was taking hold of us, a renewed interest in the verticality with which our city was defiantly surfacing from the waters. We would marvel at the way its reflection chased its real self, an upside-down version replete with seemingly endless promises of depth and continuity. The city's avenues had now turned into broad canals, and a new-found silence and quietude was spreading through them like a breeze caressing our faces, especially in those scarlet summer evenings when even the few remaining birds would stand still and watch. Rare moments of collective desire, these, with some west-facing terraces and balconies across the city appropriated as new public spaces, filling with people from all floors and of all provenances, drinks in hand, chatting away.

These were early days. In the back of our minds we were all pretending to be passengers onboard a large cruiser, moving into the future with an imperious deliberateness so that not a single drop of our drinks would ever be unnecessarily spilt and thereby add to the fatal liquid slowness lurking below us.

## four

In those early days, when we still did not know how long the waters were going to stay, the few surviving cafés and restaurants moved up to the open roof-top terraces. Those usually drab and neglected spaces were being rapidly spruced up and, riding that wave of denial that seemed to have settled on the city, were promising carefree evenings. The new marketing campaigns of these high-end pop-up establishments were now focussed on the views offered, presenting the whole visit as a playful new experience of looking at the flooded city from on high.

Something that the marketing campaigns were keen on hiding was that these restaurants and upmarket cafés would often share the roof space with whoever had been displaced and failed to secure better accommodation. Roofs were being rapidly taken over by anyone who could get to them, in an attempt to stay dry. White linen, silver cutlery, and table service was often taking place next to rickety tents and sleep ing bags spread around large open spaces, with children running between the tables and parents chasing after them as the restaurant-goers tried to cast the children a faux polite smile between bites. But this is how things were: the humidity had made it impera tive that people seek the higher terraces, whether for setting up home or having candlelit suppers.

It is true that people were mostly eager to reinforce the stereotypes with which they regarded each oth er. But a stunned version of social tourism was also on the rise: people who never mixed before now had the opportunity to see each other in a new and more clement light. Attempts at dividing the space with potted plants and other fence-like contraptions that blocked the view from outside were quickly taken apart by both sides: everyone wanted a piece of these new vistas populated by unfamiliar types of people and these alien everyday rites taking place against the backdrop of the flooded city. This soon turned out to be a selling point for many of these restaurants, which emphasised in their advertisements the unexpected social aspect of 'making new friends' while sipping your vintage port.

A tentative, random democracy of sorts, as if the flatness of the water below was rubbing off on the skin of the residents, making them more open, more curious, perhaps—certainly more available to the gaze of the other. No one could tell how long this was going to last.

## five

A couple of families moved to our floor. One of them took up the flat of a man we knew by sight, a banker or something. We don't know how they got access to it, or what their connection was to the previous owner whom anyway we had not seen since the rising of the waters. There might not have been one—property was becoming scarce, but at the same time somewhat more readily up for grabs. Squatting was slowly becoming standard practice, although it was much less acceptable if the previous occupiers had actually been physically displaced. This was hard to prove, though, and the police (or whatever counted as police in those days) did not much care about who occupied what, as long as the available flats across the city were fully occupied and homelessness was contained.

Selina, the woman of the family that moved in next door, was very friendly. She invited us over to their new place, a flat we had never seen from the inside. We welcomed the opportunity despite our initial misgivings about sanctioning what we thought was essentially a break-in. We were, perhaps inevitably, identifying with the previous owners, who, although this was by no means certain, could have returned at some point and discovered that their property was no longer theirs. It may have been at that time that the habits of most people, even the ones who had recently occupied a new space—especially them—started changing. We began spending much longer in our flats than before the waters, perhaps afraid of going for an evening out and coming back to find new occupiers settled in their homes. On the other hand, we understood the need for property to be used and for people to inhabit structurally sound and dry quarters. Day by day we were becoming more liquid-like, understanding the need to fill up every available space, often indiscriminately, ignoring the usual doors and walls. Just like the water, we too were rising and spreading, flowing together or quickening into whirlpools of conflict.

The flat showed signs of the kind of predicament wherein the taste and social class of the new occupiers differed radically from those of the previous owners. The standard minimalist original building design was taken over by a functional approach, with surfaces being used for actually putting things on and walls for sticking up photographs and posters. The new family had managed to make it look quite homely and personal, helped by the fact that they seemed to have brought with them a great deal of stuff from their previous residence. We were welcomed in by Selina's large, open smile and proudly ushered towards the windows from where we could admire the view. The flat was on the west side of the building and their view was different to ours, bringing in a city that glimmered in the late afternoon light. We were appropriately complimentary and repeatedly commented on how they must come over too to see our view, how different it was: we're sure you will find it interesting, although not as open as yours. These overdrive moments of civic normality were quickly becoming the new expected behaviour all over the city, with any trace of irony meticulously avoided.

We were then shown to the table, its dark glass surface partly covered by a soft, flowery tablecloth overflowing with cups, jars, plates of biscuits, sliced cakes, and savoury snacks. Her husband and their son also joined in. They were distinctly less friendly and somehow broody, as if they wanted to show us that we were now invading their space and time. We took our places hesitantly, trying a little too enthusiastically to focus on Selina's chatting while visually blocking the son and the father. But we were all too aware of the dark silences that were sliding amongst us, threatening even Selina's seemingly inexhaustible arsenal of badinage. For our part, we asked several questions in order to keep the conversation going, but it was hard to do so in an interesting way: we could never ask anything about their past, how they ended up on our floor, where they were before that, what they did in their lives. All these felt out of bounds, somehow implying that this newly arrived family did not belong here, that they were still outsiders. We could only make the smallest of small talk, and this relied on a sense of the necessity of proving that everything was normal.

But there were moments when even that sense of necessity collapsed. Then the silences would seep in. And, unlike the fairly harmless silences that might befall a dinner party with newly acquainted guests, or even the embarrassed silence that follows a social faux pas, these new silences, so much more frequent and inevitable since the waters, had become viscous and hefty. It was as if they had a different consistency, as if they were made up of weightier molecules floating around us, as if they were breathing heavier breaths full of sticky humidity. We could *hear* the silence much more clearly now, almost bouncing on the surface of the water below and doubling its own gelatinous elasticity. And then the silence would become a threatening alterity sliding over our skins like somebody else's sweat, bearing a scent that none of us could recognise.

# six

*A few years before the waters.*

You got us in the habit of going for a swim at the local swimming pool every Saturday. It was a pool like any other municipal pool, a bit too busy, a bit unkempt but quite jolly. The only thing neither of us liked was the occasional competitive surge that would take over the crowd and, as if by contagion, make us all swim faster, keeping fastidiously to our lanes and quickly forgetting how to dither or play. We would only re-alise afterwards that we too had been taken over by it—our breaths shallower and our limbs tenser in the showers. There was an elation that went with it, an illusion of fearless progress that pushed us to follow everyone else in the false belief that we were leading. Our side-glances at the stragglers only confirmed our aquatic superiority, making us go faster with every arm spread, adjusting and readjusting our goals for yet another length, yet another spectacularly swift and elegant turn. But even while we were performing these dolphin-like acrobatics, secure in the sense of our nascent amphibianism, wrapped in a water that made us feel safe and victorious, we knew that this was not the water we desired.

You had the idea, one warm morning just before our usual pool time, to go to a pond in the nearby park. You did not say why exactly, perhaps you did not know either. I thought it just would be a short walk, perhaps with a coffee at the park café, but you insisted that we take our pool bags with us as if we were going to the swimming pool. For a moment I had the impression that you were planning a swim there—quite a ridiculous idea given the nature of the water, its shallowness, its ecology. But some-thing else came up as we approached the pond: a notion that felt like a shared emergence, a common plan solid in its unspokenness.

We knelt by the side of the pond, feet on the hard cement edge that stopped water and reeds from invading the rest of the park. We leaned carefully towards the green water, just enough to see our faces reflected on its surface. We pulled out from our satchels the plastic carrier bags we always carried with us when going to the swimming pool to put our wet swimming trunks in after the swim. They were small and quite flimsy. We dipped them in the pond water and filled them up enough to create two small round baubles of distended plastic film, securely knotted in by the ends of the bag. We then helped each other, securing the little baubles on each other's wrists by tying up the flapping handles like kids do with their balloons. We walked slowly towards the swimming pool, feeling the weight of our liquid balloons dangling on our wrists. Rather than pulling our arms skywards, they plopped about our bodies, bouncing softly in a reminder of a gravity as playful as it was inevitable.

We felt silly, especially when entering the swimming pool with our plastic baubles awkwardly attached to our wrists. But we also felt united by a strange confession, joined in a necessity that was simultaneously plunging us deeper into the swimming pool and keeping us apart from it, as if we were floating just above its chlorinated surface. Our swimming technique was impaired, of course, made cumbersome by the bouncing bags awkwardly splashing against the surface of the water and increasing its resistance to our movements. I was afraid that they might tear and that the pond water would pour out and mix unhygienically with the swimming water. I was terrified at the thought that a change of pool colour might happen, leaving us both utterly exposed, as if it were our bodies themselves that were leaking illicit liquids. The following Saturday, and all the Saturdays after that, we took with us pharmacy carrier bags that looked more resilient, more ready to accommodate our other waters.

It is such a bore when you study my comings and goings, jotting them down to catch me next time. Look at you, drunk with power, enclosing me, channelling me, controlling me, putting me in narrow waterways or large deposits, trapping me in reservoirs, framing me behind long dams or in tiny tubes.

No, you don't understand—you don't hurt me, you *cannot* hurt me.

It is your attitude that irritates me, that bossy, pitiable, macho egomania with which you think you can control me, and your automatic tendency to measure me: weight, speed, density, frequency.

Yeah fine, carry on, see if I care.

Human rhythms are so shallow I can barely feel them. They ride a different temporality than I do: day and night, forgettably short seasons, unregistrable epochs.

Ebb and flow, streams and currents, waves and tsunamis: you want me to conform to what you think my rhythms are—see how you can never see beyond your little selves?—a breath of rising and falling, a living regularity because life is regular and water is life, right?

OK. But you really ought to know—well you do not *need* to, I do not even think you *can* know, but it is good sometimes to show you that you cannot know—anyway, you really should try to understand that my breath is not of your life, or of any life.

My breath is time.

My breath is of a universe that hosts me in globular suspension between planets, in vast clouds of a rain that will never fall, in fathomless oceans suspended in space and floating about unsupported: my breath is there, rounded up in a water that you will never drink.

My breath is polarised, spread across aeons, breathing in when nothing was impossible and breathing out when the possibilities will have shut forever.

But, OK, you cannot conceive this.

Let's focus on your planet, that hydrospheric apparition on stilts in the great hall of cosmic gossip. Even then, you think of me as percentages: oh wow so much of the surface of the earth, no really, so much of a human body. Eye rolling stuff.

Just shut up and listen for a moment and you might just about understand that my breath is caught in the rattle of a dying sun, hidden under strata of a geology that ignores you, deep in the centre of what you call your planet and with whose body you will never manage to sleep.

My breath is liquidity in waiting, tangled with chunks of eternity.

## seven

In time, time also changed. It became slower and hazier. Accuracy was no longer a possibility, and the city started moving in rhythms of approximation and contingency. The boats provided by the city council were never enough, so we had to find other ways of dealing with our transport needs. The frequently insuperable difficulty of getting around meant that even those of us who could afford it had generally stopped moving about much unless it was absolutely necessary, and even then we could never guarantee that we would be on time. People extended their everyday activities on previously underused balconies, windowsills and corridors.

It was this generalised inward turning that forced buildings to become as self-sufficient as possible, utilising whatever expertise their residents could offer. The rooftop restaurants and cafés started shutting down for lack of clients and of raw materials for elaborate dishes and cocktails. Many of the shops that had opened on the third and fourth floors were also closing, unless they were providing for their neighbours' immediate needs of food and basic sustenance. Hordes of delivery people on makeshift motorboats initially criss-crossed the canals, creating a constant buzz in the city. But even these started to abate: since internet access was no longer reliable, online transactions could not be trusted; petrol was becoming an inflated commodity; and delivery charges were mounting. The most entrepreneurial of us became small-scale itinerant salespeople, buying or hiring boats and moving from building to building, buying and selling stuff for money or exchanging it for other goods. But because boats were becoming a rare commodity, when need urged, forgotten children's canoes, old wardrobes, even simple plywood doors were dug up and thrown in the water in the hope that they would float. And, in general, they did. Distances were navigable, the waters were smooth, and since few of us really knew what we were doing, speeds were tentative even for those who had the good fortune of possessing a vessel with an engine.

In the places where buildings were close to each other, planks were installed, jutting out of windows and doors and linking up whole areas in a network of walkable highways. Buildings became tentacled, linked to their surroundings in a promising and seemingly well-ordered web of routes, yet often leading nowhere near where one would ideally like to end up despite appearances to the contrary. Some shop owners got organised and tried to set up an ambitious network of planks linking the third and fourth floors of various blocks, but the maintenance was so complex that few parts of the network survived more than a couple of months. Still, when these planks started being installed, it was bracing to see, especially early in the morning, rows of people patiently queueing up in single rows, trying to reach nearby buildings. Some would carry on going to their work like this, if their workplace was on a walkable route; others would visit friends or do their shopping or avail themselves of whatever was left of the city's services; and others would come out seemingly determined and busy but in reality simply rushing out of their homes in an often pointless attempt to reestablish normality through a morning constitutional or by mingling with other people.

As a last resort, some people swam, defying the risks of infection or the very real chance of impaling themselves on a protruding piece of metal lying invisible just below the surface. But the ones who swam seemed to have traced their routes carefully, avoiding at least the predictable risks. Some of them would also dive, often disappearing from view midswim, and going as deep as they could. They were part of this new generation of inverted climbers,

climbers that dived rather than ascended, holding onto trees that were not yet uprooted, railings that had not yet detached from facades, streetlights that were still standing in their recently discovered darkness. It was said that these diving climbers would go as low as the old basements of the city, out of nostalgia or perhaps an emerging desire to develop larger breathing capacities that would allow them to stay underwater for longer. Rumours had started even then that some of them were well on their way to building a life right there, on the urban seabed.

# eight

We didn't know how long the waters were going to stay, or whether they were going to rise further. Predictions were largely unscientific and unreliable since most of the measuring equipment was damaged and, one after the other, the usual channels of communication were inexorably coming down. Rumours circulated about an imminent withdrawal of the waters, but the reasons supporting such rumours were tenuous to say the least.

Initially, most people tried to find answers outside. All airfields were flooded, all roads submerged, so the only way out of the city was through water. All the large ships that used to be accessible to the city's residents seemed to have sailed away, probably loaded with those amongst us who wanted to leave and could afford to pay extortionately high prices for a passage to no one knew where. Amongst those that remained, a new group of people emerged: well-organised, deeply determined, and confident pioneers of the dry, teams brimming with hope and the ambition to become our city's explorers and to return loaded with goods from our past and answers for our future. Rage against the waters and the hope of discovering those parts of the planet that had not turned against us seemed to be propelling these dry-land crusaders ever further away from the city.

Of those who had left shortly after the waters, most never made it back. We allowed ourselves to believe that the departing ones were setting up home somewhere there, but most of us were too doubtful to take the risk and follow. The few who did return brought with them only rumours rather than actual experiences, stories that would become the subject of corridor gossip however monstrously untrue or even contradictory. But these stories managed to keep alive the hope of a better world outside: floating colonies for the super-rich, vast indifferent arks gleamingly passing by, never stopping for anything or anyone; vertical structures piling up millions of displaced people, reaching sky high and oscillating wildly with every little gust of wind; and even dry high grounds, promised lands where everyone lived in peace, where farm animals were still alive and crops still offered the old food staples.

And then there were others—devoid of heroism and without a thought of crusading glory—who would just climb on a raft, often in the middle of the night, and start rowing across the water boulevards and floating above the outer suburbs, most of which were almost entirely submerged. People spoke of endless rows of low houses and of gardens now colonised by the vegetal and marine life that was taking over the city. These rows were interrupted only by the occasional taller building or by still-standing monuments incongruously protruding from those infinite lagunas of the periphery. The suburban populations had long gone, large chunks of them having escaped the waters and moved into the vacated upper floors of the central buildings. Yet there were quite a few unlucky ones who drowned in their sleep, either unaware of the rising water or fighting not to lose one another or their belongings. There was nothing to see and do there anymore, just a passage towards an imagined dry world outside.

Cinder, Selina's broody young son whom we often met in our floor's corridor, was one of those castrated pioneers, eager to encounter the dry old world and leave behind our current humid existence. His mother kept saying that she really wished he wouldn't go, but his response was always the same: he had no choice. He was battling claustrophobia and social isolation of a kind he had never experienced before. He was used to being connected with his peers, mostly electronically but also in the neighbourhood where they lived before moving to ours, and neither of these means of connection was any longer readily available. The internet was erratic to say the least, and one by one most areas seemed to be switching off. As for the streets, this was hardly a term we could use anymore.

Cinder returned after only a few days in the open laguna. He encountered nothing but endless horizontality, an infinity of wet reflecting surfaces on which to marvel at his solitude, sparsely pierced by isolated and inhospitable structures and traversed only by other pioneers of the dry at various points on the spectrum between hope and despair. In the weeks following his return, although he wasn't any friendlier, he seemed calmer, as if he had finally put to rest a thought that had been tormenting him. He even spoke to us at some length about his journey outside that one time we met him next to the no-longer-working lift. He mostly talked about what he ate when he was out there, about the fish he managed to catch and how it tasted funny and he had to cast it back in. He also spoke of the sun, constantly refracted behind humid columns of clouds rising from the water and making navigation even harder. But he was speaking with a composure that lacked any sign of his usual edge. When we asked him about new friends in the neighbourhood, he just shrugged.

So we knew very little with any certainty. One thing, though, was confirmed by everyone: that we were not the only ones flooded. For all we knew, every city across the globe had suffered a comparable fate. Even the mountains, invisible from within the city but appearing like giant glaciers as soon as one started navigating a little further out, seemed to be under the same level of water wherever one went. There was no convincing explanation for the flooding, except perhaps for a change in the earth's magnetic field exacerbated by an anthropogenic attrition that was playing havoc with gravity, making the whole globe a laguna of (relatively speaking) shallow water swamping the horizon.

Traditional religious explanations sputtered out quickly since the waters seemed neither to recede nor to bloat further, forcing the various religious leaders and believers to concede that, whatever apocalypse this was, it was fairly flat and unwrathful. Different metaphysical explanations started emerging, initially at least, providing succour to those who were desperately seeking an answer: the most talked-about in the city was that the waters were a sort of protective layer of jellied skin, a kind of planetary defence mechanism that shielded the earth from the noxious solar radiation outside while at the same time drowning off the otherwise unstoppable human presence. As a result of this, some people started counting time in reverse, with date zero being the moment at which the waters would reach that specific mark on that specific wall, or the city's final collapse, or human extinction, or even the earth's resurrection. They introduced in this way a host of microcalendars that made any arrangement a long-drawn-out affair of multiple clarifications.

## waterspeak

But possibly the most exasperating thing you do is
deifying me.

You want me to be your life and death, sin and
cleansing, purity and pollution.

And then you stuff me with all sorts of rubbish:
you throw into me your newborn and your newly
dead, hoping that I will conduct them closer to your
divinities. You dip your arks in me and think that
all will be sorted, that the future will be purified.
You wash your limbs and pray, because you think
I can mediate between your filth and your holi-
ness. You even bottle me up like some sort of genie,
carrying me around for impromptu exorcisms and
other small, everyday god-caressing necessities.

Oh how I hate this—your desperate attempt at understanding me amounts either to chopping me up
in little containers or to making me a god.

You are drowning yourselves in your font of knowledge.

I mean, you and causality are such bananas. It
would be a bizarre world if causality worked
like this: someone places a monster amongst my
waves—
a terrifying kraken shaking the seas, or a sluicing
sea serpent coiling up storms—and boom, waves
swell, seas bloat, storms are cooked.

If only!

So, what if your Poseidon shakes his trident and
your Hydra screams with all her heads? What if
your Ran sucks in everyone, your Tipua roars from
the depths of my stomach, your Tiamat copulates

with stinky Abzu to spit out a cluster of rheostating
gods controlling your very own bodies? All these
looming Leviathans that supposedly nestle in me
but were in reality just conjured up by your gory
imagination: your little omnipotent palisades of
self-torture.

Even your crazy plastic excreta poured out of your
civilised stomata that reek of self-importance are
not enough to pull my causal strings.

All these failed ways of dealing with your inca-
pacity. Can you see me yawn? Ah! the waters part,
miracle—well. No. I am yawning. This is simple,
irritable boredom.

Well, you can keep your Ras and Aquariuses,
your Scyllas and even your Aphrodites, 'cause I am
gobbing them out now, one by one, splatting them
on your faces, tears for the end of creation.

# nine

People were disappearing all the time. The whole city was much quieter, not just because of the absence of cars and the muffling effect of the water, but also because the city was progressively emptying out, draining of human life and its movement. Or simply absorbing it, like a towel absorbs the excess. Death became our natural bedfellow. It felt like a cull, indomitable and abrupt, especially at the beginning when no one knew how to protect themselves. Drowning was the first and most direct cause of death, with people vanishing while sleeping or having their dinner, in sudden floods caused by minor collapses or by movements between walls. Things were thought sturdy and watertight until a raging chamber tsunami would swell up. Then there was polluted water, taps spitting miasma that looked and smelled like pure water and caught one unawares, drinks made with water that had come too close to burst sewers, or even hot drinks that did not quite reach the level of heat sufficient to kill the bacteria.

And then, there were the suicides. Spectacular hurtlings out of flats and straight onto the sharp debris of the waters below, discreet phials of hard-to-find expensive poisons sourced from sewers and promising swift oblivion, or plungings into extremely cold water that brought the human body to a cerulean shutdown. Nearly all suicides had to do with water. In a warped circle of brutal generosity, the thing that pushed us to kill ourselves was also offering the means of doing it.

Some of our neighbours would disappear in their own apartments, going deep into their rooms, withdrawing from the world, shutting down. A woman who had always lived alone just above us seemed to be heading in that direction. We visited her often, especially after we realised that she wasn't faring so well. We would bring her food or an old magazine we had already read too many times, or a piece of news about the building or the weather, or whatever we could in order to make her come to the door. But she soon stopped doing even that and our knocks would go unheeded. Next thing we heard, somebody had moved into her apartment. We felt lonely after that, heavy with guilt, drowning in complicity. And yet, we forgot.

And then there was a host of other causes, some more conjectural than others: toxic fish, poisoned bird meat, rotten antediluvian foodstuffs, liquification of the mind, air so thick with water that it stopped people from breathing and suffocated them in their sleep, or water sprees that ran amok haunting whole buildings and driving their residents against each other in horrific bouts of violence.

Then there were those who sank deeper in. Rumours about the diving climbers were by now proliferating, lithe swimmers growing gills and scales or lithe roots and anemone-like heads, and becoming one with this new planet. If they did exist, they were entirely caught up in their precipitative evolutionary whirlwind and presumably busy with learning how not to mind the loss of their legs or their hearing—since they were constantly plunged into frothy rapids—or their vision, which would have increasingly resembled the rain-strewn windows of cataract sufferers. But of all these new things, one would imagine that perhaps the hardest to get used to would have been a permanent sense of asphyxia, as if a ceiling had been placed over the entire earth and the air could no longer circulate— an undying death or a life that would have seemed to teeter constantly on the edge of its end.

But perhaps these stories were just fables we were telling each other, projections of our own de-sires, romantically overblown to appeal to our self-importance. Our remarkable adaptability, our astonishing survival skills, our species' pride, our trust in technology: all of these were planks onto which we grabbed as everything around us was sinking. In a way, they were more believable than the promises of dry land and floating colonies brought to us by the pioneers. Yet they all served the same purpose: to dissimulate what was actually happening to all of us. We were all changing, turning inside as if preparing for a long winter sleep.

We never seriously considered leaving, despite being plunged into an irreversible period of slow-brewing panic and sadness about the loss of life around us. After the breakdown of public transport, we had stopped seeing those friends and relatives that lived outside our immediate vicinity. We kept on wondering whether they were still alive. At the beginning, we were desperately asking for news about them, so much so that any meeting with friends or even mere acquaintances was now reduced to a manic exchange of information about people we had in common. But little by little, this habit fizzled out, just as the trickle of news began to dry out. Our social life was being narrowed down to the neighbourhood—but even that had changed. We no longer saw the people we used to see on the street and whose habits we had got to know. Most of them had left, died, or simply vanished, and had progressively been replaced by the new people who moved to the vacated flats. It wasn't just human life that was being lost. With the exception of seagulls, a few old and some new fish species, and some amphibian reptiles that were obviously proliferating, the only other species left were stressed pets, clouds of insects, and gargantuan, ever-expanding water plants. Our sole way to deal with this relentless loss is by turning inside, deeper into ourselves and our immediate beloved ones.

We used to say that we would leave when all this death and disappearance around us became unbearable.

But it never did. It managed instead to insert itself in our everyday experience like an almost-natural inevitability. We came to realise that it was only with a great deal of artifice that we had so far managed to stall this lethal galloping in our lives. News about a friend or a neighbour's death would initially leave us shaken, with fear for our own lives haunting our days and nights. But in time we were simply nodding in resignation: another drop in that already overflowing lake of sadness that we learned to call the present. We even got used to seeing corpses floating by in front of our windows—languid, unhurried, almost grand in their final parade. It was a sad state of affairs when we had to admit that we were no longer particularly traumatised by such occurrences, when we stopped calling each other to come to the window to share our horror.

We kept on setting ourselves movable deadlines, events after which we could not possibly carry on staying. Some of them were silly, like when we used to say that we would leave when the last TV station shut down. But we stayed even when the TV started obsessively showing the same episodes of a reality show we had seen years ago, always the same two episodes, something about a house eviction and a rowdy crowd thirsty for public humiliation, one after the other, back-to-back over endless twenty-four-hour shifts, as if the only thing of relevance was the escape from that televised household.

And then we said we would leave when the radio would fall silent. But we did not even realise when this actually happened, until one day we trailed the airwaves and encountered nothing but the noise of emptiness that was remarkably similar to that of the waters beneath us on a windy night. Then we said, we will leave when there is no longer any internet, or when we see the final public transport boat sail away, or when we run out of money and things to exchange. Or when crime becomes too much, or when water, and then electricity, get cut off. But we endured all that and much more. We got used to the brutality with which social bonds were being severed, and the insecurity generated by the almost complete disintegration of networks and social reliances. We even got used to ignoring our ever-further postponed deadlines of departure, until one day we said, we are staying.

Perhaps we were becoming aware that, with each new strike, we were simply adapting to a life that, although apparently much harder, was in reality merely different. Or perhaps we were hypnotised by this aquatic city, by the imposed slowness, the inevitable lassitude that was bubbling up from within its shifting foundations. We felt bound to it by an umbilical cord that no one had the power to bite off. And so we curved inward and became soft, round bubbles of air contained by this immense urban womb.

## ten

Lorna used to manage the local supermarket before the waters. It was a small one, more corner-shop than proper supermarket, part of a co-operative chain with its own products alongside the more mainstream ones on the shelves. What made it slightly different was its small but capacious gardening corner, clearly catering to the interests of the locals whose blooming back gardens, verandas, and windowsills were considered part of the area's charm. The original shop was not in our building, but for some reason Lorna moved her business into ours, taking up a sprawling, awkwardly-shaped flat on the fourth floor that had recently been vacated by its owners. Marek, one of the employees who used to do the late shift, joined her, and the two together managed to open shop, bringing down most of the internal walls, boarding up some of the windows, and opening up a rather roughly cut hole in the side of the corridor in a semblance of a shop window.

They initially placed some tins and cleaning goods on the rickety shelves that they managed to mount across the opening. But this makeshift shop window worked more as a melancholy reminder that life had changed irreversibly than a true advertisement of what was inside. Eventually they realised this too, since the corridor window was progressively taken over by sprawling greenery—initially accompanied by a couple of gardening tools and some seed envelopes with pictures of colourful blooms, and then by a hesitant actual pot with seedlings aided by artificial light, until it finally became a verdant explosion that reached out across the corridor's walls to create a branched-out bower, a simulation of nature's awnings conveniently laid out for romantic promenades and adolescent trysts. But this rewilding wasn't just happening at the shop window. The outside reflected what was happening inside the shop. Tuna tins and packets of crisps were being steadily replaced by hyssops and irises, strawberry bushes and ivies, hydrangeas, willow oaks and magnolias, and even a (comparably speaking) small weeping willow that—placed as it was between the old rooms, just where a wall used to stand—was growing so prodigiously that it had taken up most of the available space, forcing everyone to walk around it and to step gingerly through its streaming long branches, which reached the by now constantly wet floor carpet. In time, this hydrophilous forest took over all the available neighbouring flats and practically converted the entire floor into a jungle, with its heavy nocturnal smells radiating from its thickets and percolating to the floors above.

People never questioned the move from the usual supermarket fare to plants, possibly because Lorna seemed to time the decline of tinned and wrapped goods with a corresponding increase in the production of tomatoes, cucumbers, salads, berries, and even some figs that she managed to grow for selling or exchanging—all the time giving away seeds for people to grow on their terraces and windowsills. Another reason for this meek acceptance might have been the fact that everyone was encouraged just to visit and wander around in what was becoming an out-of-control green sprawl, a sprawl that was eating up the old flat's layout and replacing it with narrow passages, low awnings, and clandestine windows to other, equally green, endlessly meandering, self-reproducing, and fractally unfolding lush rooms that were formed solely of trunks, branches, and foliage. A visit to Lorna's was always a folding-in moment, a home away from home or perhaps a shell away from our own flat shells, a duplication of the womb that we were all seeking in various ways in our lives. We were told that people willingly got lost in the exponentially growing and almost unexplorable urban garden, and Lorna and Marek would leave them undisturbed, diligently pulling the heavy night doors shut, walling them in for a few more hours of hypnotised, quiet joy.

Apart from allowing their shop to become a common space for all, with them being the tutelar curators rather than in any way the owners of a property, Lorna and Marek engaged in yet another, even stranger activity that also catered to our needs. One evening, when the greening of the shop was still at its early stages, Marek mentioned how, to start with, Lorna could not swim and how Marek had done most of the diving into the lower levels of the city where the old shop was, in order to source whatever salvageable products he could. Soon, however, with Marek's guidance, Lorna started diving too. Her perseverance was only tempered by a residual fear of drowning that never quite left her. The fear was making her gestures unnecessarily strenuous and her breathing fast and excessively shallow. She would often then enter a state of underwater somnambulism, as breathless as it was fearless, unconsciously moving about the submerged supermarket aisles and invariably ending up at the small gardening corner at the rear entrance of the shop.

While initially Marek would emerge laden with the products they had agreed that they most needed, Lorna would be seen emerging perched on giant clay pots, entangled with drowned roots and overwatered branches heavy with their seemingly irrepressible will to adapt. Regaining consciousness, Lorna would always be surprised by her loot, but would nevertheless set to work, planting the seeds in the shop and hoping for eventual growth. Marek started to follow suit, bringing up more and more plants apparently without wondering how it was that the little gardening corner could keep on providing so generously. But he could never do it the way Lorna did, losing himself on that plane of existence where breath was no longer the first necessity. And so he would often be alone in the new shop, serving customers and winking knowingly at our occasional questions about Lorna's whereabouts.

# waterspeak

You know I don't speak, don't you?

How do you feel about hearing your own voice,
booming vicariously in your mind, thinking that it
is me?

You are borrowing again from my munificence.
Can you feel the strings puppeteering you through
the pages? And to think I do not even have arms.

Such parasites. Always bound by your presence, yet
miraculously always missing out on the present—
how on earth do you manage that!

It's all about you, isn't it? Like when you think I
work against you, torturing your bodies and tormenting your souls—yes, all those clichés. Big
waves: oh, volatile, threatening, angry, malevolent,
vengeful thing this water, man-eater really, etc.
Lapping wavelets: ah, so welcoming, peaceful, meditative, in sync with the universe, bring those soy
candles out.

You count waves to sleep; you count oceans as if
they were human syncopated breaths

But if you were to propel yourselves a little out of
your orbit to see time for what it is, if you were able
even for a flash to rush through aeons and stellar
deaths as I do, you might see me carving the Grand
Canyon in an instant of capillary ennui, or falling
on your planet's surface for centuries—continuous-
ly, relentlessly, a cataclysm to drown all cataclysms
that just a few moments later made you stand up
and say hi.

Your take on all this is so stuffy, you make me
weep! You put it in little books and claim the moral

importance of its truth: you have been a bad boy, have some flooding to sort you out.

Yeah, none of that. Sorry to bang on about it like this but causality ain't anthropocentric.

I know how hard it is for you to tolerate indifference. But that's how I feel about you.

*A few years before the waters.*

The height of our love came shortly after the usual waves of raw desire subsided. Still there of course, potently present but somehow softer, less urgent, this desire was slowly being replaced by another desire: I seemed always to want a deeper connection with you. A thirst for more—quantity and quality, broader and ampler, sharp yet unfocussed, unquenchable by an easy or even laboured orgasm—meant that I was reluctant to let you do anything on your own for long, that I was constantly fighting the urge to text or call or even drop everything and come and find you wherever you might be.

It was hard to do this elegantly. Sexual desire was fine, often wordless, using long-established codes. But this was too exposing. It demanded a riskier funambulism, a deeper plunge into my insecurities. I was sometimes swallowed up by an urge—where was it coming from, was this really me? It felt so alien, an urge to be loved to the point of suffocation, and I was often fumbling in the dark, wondering whether I was offering too much, whether I was spreading my love too thickly and running the risk of your getting fed up. But you never reacted restlessly or impatiently. No, you would always reciprocate and often initiate this obsessive pavane we had started dancing around each other, an emollient to my fear.

The strange thing, however, was the timing. While I did constantly desire contact, I did not always want to act upon it. Not that I loved you any less or needed you any differently during those times. I just did not bring myself to initiate any contact, whether that meant coming over to the sofa to sit with you or taking your hand and holding it or texting you the simple code word that meant 'I love you' or 'I am thinking of you' or something to that effect, an odd little word that had emerged between us, who knows how? Neither of us remembers with certainty, and no one else could possibly understand what the connection of this strange little word to any amorous emotions might be. Anyway, there is this word, and so many little variations and even relevant emojis—babyspeak of sorts that enabled a flow of unweighty but candid communication between us that punctured our day at various unexpected points. But there were times when even that word was not tempting—I liked the idea of its being there, a familiar nest of tenderness between us, without the need for us to visit it. At those times, when a sense of contentment and a desire for boundary-setting between us—feeble as it may have been—was making me take a notional distance from you, I noticed that you were the one who initiated the communication. It was as if you were sniffing out my lassitude and wanted to prick my idle moment with a ping or nudge my TV watching with a caress and bring me back to our dance. I would always respond, of course, and play along, kindly and lovingly but not fully there. And at other times, when I was initiating our contact, I would feel that you were responding in the same way as I was, kind and loving but not fully there. But that was all right. I would smile knowing that something was deepening even then.

And so with our nights. We had developed this nocturnal ritual, more minuet than pavane now, where you would fall asleep and I would stay awake, looking after your breath, your covers, or your pillows, occasionally caressing your cheek, but also reading in low light next to you or just listening to your night noises. I would eventually fall asleep and that would be the signal, communicated in some sort of subaquatic mode and reaching you like a wave of a fisherman encountered in the open sea, a gesture of solidarity but also a warning: distances in the dark can be deceiving, especially on misty nights like this; do not crash against my boat, stay here but stay away as well, wake up and stay alert. And you would wake up. And then silently, in an unforced, natural manner, you would take over our vigilance, while I would slip away.

Our code word was 'ducks'. The water was implied.

My white is blue. So is my slow green, my oily black,
my spirited azure, or my dirty grey. All blue really. Whenever there is light, I catch it, play with it,
absorb it as if I needed it—why not make it happy,
light has always been a good friend, really. Even so, I
do not welcome it all. I choose only the parts I want,
picky cobalt peacock me, and then I scatter them
around like phenomenological fireworks, dot them
like big bangers on the world's retina—see how cool
I am, seamlessly moving between philosophical par-
lance and street. That's another story, another great
quality of mine. We are now talking about my colour.
So, if there is light, I reflect it all blue and cocky. If
there is no light around, I wait. Aeons of waiting,
knitwork of a universe that forgets its own self. But
light always comes. So it is blue, even when my white
mountains—ice peaks of my consistency and scraping
skies of my polar glory—glisten, slide, and melt. It is
blue when my powdery white opens up crevasses of
raw thaw, bubbling up with my seas underneath. It is
still blue when it devours your cities and your minds,
still blue when it creeps in your mouths yellow with
acid and death, gleaming like radioactive enamel
spread over your graves. It is still blue when you scatter colourful flowers amongst your floating deads. It
is blue when red with charcoal frenzy in the deepest
core of your planet, and it is blue between your tall
buildings on those hot summer evenings when even
the breath of your lover is a skin too many. It is blue
when you let yourself fly in me, cutting my globules
in thick slices, spreading your dream bodies light
and wavy across time. It is blue when caught on
the wings of a bird, and it is blue when mixed with
the green iguanas of the deep. It is blue when you
shut your eyes and it is blue when you open them.
It is blue when I rush down, shards of transparency
drumming the top of your heads like night thoughts.
And it is blue when you piss me, yellow reminders of

dehydration.  It is blue when my impasto blends the above and the below, sky and sea with their edges always deferred, steam and myopia, the curve of every star, the horizon that opens with every new wave. It is blue, that round thing that moves slowly with you balancing on its crust, a shawl of suspended lakes as deep as the weather trailing around it.

## twelve

Cinder and his father were installing some cage-like contraptions on their balcony next door. We tried to figure out what they were for, but failed, so in the end we asked them directly. They said they were bird traps. This was surprising: the majority of birds seemed to have emigrated or died out, the only exception being the seagulls that had been proliferating since the waters had risen. At all times of day and night, the city was echoing with their screams and vertiginous flights. They were becoming more and more aggressive because the food supply was disproportionate to their increased population. They were so many that one presumably only needed to walk out onto one's balcony and grab one by the neck. What to do with them, though? Cinder said that seagull meat tasted good, albeit still too fishy for him. Most available food was increasingly of that vaguely marine taste—seaweed or fish or seafood, invariably salty and of a mushy consistency. Seagull meat, on the other hand, was firm and sinewy, he said while banging on a fairly large metal cage door.

They never offered to share their cooked meat with us, despite the embarrassment of captured prey on a daily basis—perhaps because they registered our disapproval or at least our hesitation. Seagulls were feasting on the human and animal bodies that were floating freely about. It was too much to eat them—a serious health risk, even. But there was something else too, some sort of ethical code that prevented us from ever considering eating seagulls, one that had little to do with their enforced necrophagy. We never quite talked about it, but we had both watched the same documentary years ago and knew that seagulls were monogamous birds pairing up for life.

This was not some sort of moral preference for monogamy over other forms of desire. Not in practice, anyway. It was more a reaction to the new flatness all around us. A monogamous relationship seemed like a convincing vestige of the old-world order, where things were still upstanding—structured rather than resigned to the general collapse.

Why is upstanding better than horizontal? We never questioned it during the early days.

Things would change eventually. But not before our own bodies finally lay down, smooth against the flatness. Until then, our horizon felt so asphyxiatingly close that it had practically enveloped us in one single fold. Our movement, our breath, our dreaming were all flooded by an insatiable horizontality. Nothing to hold onto, nothing to look up to. The only thing interrupting this flatness was the verticality of the buildings that we inhabited—and to this we subconsciously added the vertiginous flights of the seagulls diving for food. These were our notional vertical lines drawn against the wet horizon. The idea of a bird pairing up for life with its partner, the toil of this airborne monogamy, made unexpected sense. It introduced into the surrounding flatness a rupture, as sharp as a shriek, as precarious as a flight.

We identified with these vertical lines and wanted desperately to reproduce them in our personal and social lives. We clung onto them as if they were life-buoys, although we could feel their hissing deflation beneath our palms.

That was the time when everything around us was becoming a metaphor.

## thirteen

*A few years before the waters.*

We were almost at the end of our first ever holiday together. We walked down to our usual end of the beach and found ourselves an empty spot by the sea.

At some point in the late afternoon, we heard screams. We sat up, books sliding down from their idle spread on our bellies, hats falling off our heads, hands shading our eyes as we tried to find out what was happening. We initially thought that the screams were coming from a baby, except that there was something unearthly about them, odd enough to yank us out of our slumber. We couldn't locate their source, and the more we looked around, the more plangent and urgent the screams became. We instinctively followed the direction of the gaze of the people around us, but whatever it was must have been happening at some point below our sightline, covered up by beach umbrellas and glistening bodies.

You stood up while I remained seated, stretching my back as far upright as I could in order to see. You seemed to have finally found out what the source of the shrieks was because your whole body shifted: you stood on your heels in a dismayed but persistent tension, raised your shoulders like a cat in defence, and jerked your head backwards in disbelief. You even stretched your arms a little and, ever so slightly, turned your upper body away from the spectacle so that, frozen in time, your posture looked out of place on that beach. You were like a figure out of a mannerist painting, filled with incongruent pathos, contorted in some sort of impossible twist, escaping yet at the same time wanting to stay put. I was transfixed by your body as it was shaped by the piercing cries, invisible arrows targeting a godless Sebastian, so much so that my desire to discover the source of the cries was diminished and I was content to observe the way in which the violence of whatever it was that you were watching was being inscribed on your body.

But I was not spared the spectacle after all. A mass of blood and cracked bones rose from the beach, all aflutter and leaky. A seagull was holding in its beak another bird, or whatever was left of it, the two of them taking off over the flat, reflecting sea in a lithe yet somewhat unsteady flight. It would seem, however, that there was still some unwanted life in the attacked body because the seagull all of a sudden interrupted its ascent, floated in mid-air for a couple of seconds, and then started dropping its weight almost vertically, as if sliding down an air shaft so narrow that it had no other choice but to fall into it. The seagull plunged into the sea beak-first. It stayed half-submerged, producing a thick quantity of froth with its beating wings, and then rose again—an elegant ellipsis carved against the midday sun—only to plunge back again with what seemed like increasing ferocity. It was clear that the seagull was trying to drown the other bird. Or perhaps it was only toying with it, wrapping itself in a spectacle of such power and control, so superior to whatever the caught bird could have ever mustered, so disproportionate and frankly unnecessary, that it felt as if the seagull was doing it all for us, its stunned, captive audience.

This seesaw was repeated a few times further, and in the process the seagull merging with the—by now no doubt—dead bird into one fiery blood clot, glistening with sea water and half eaten flesh. The spectacle was even more paralysing because it was unfolding in total silence, its echoes strikingly empty after the terrifying shrieks. The violence was muted to a meteorology of falling bodies: the screams had been replaced by the thud of bodies breaking the surface of the water, as loud and disconnected as if a taut forearm was repeatedly fisting the sea. The plunging mass finally moved away, dripping water in long rivulets that caught the sun in an invitation to follow, and everything tried to go back to normal, which largely involved consoling the kids that had either been scared or overly excited by the spectacle.

You remained standing, still half-turned away but slowly extricating yourself from your pose, your shoulders morphing into a shrug, your head into a riotous laugh, even your arms—initially opened up in a plea—now rushed to meet each other in order to applaud: an appreciative spectator of the acrobatic display that had taken place before you.

How did we manage to keep on watching? Why did we never think to do something about it? Even avert our gaze. Why this fascination?

I thought I would never understand it. Yet now that our world is surrounded by indomitable violence, I have begun to understand this paradox. We are all complicit, whether we keep on watching or not.

How can such violence occur when the sea is so calm, when the clouds have rested for the day, when the lightly saline breeze touches your bodies in such a gentle way? Shocking, right? Yep, I am being sarcastic.

But see how I am being used in the most shameless of ways to justify your surprise at reality?

Let's put the record straight: I give this planet its weather. But then you're messing it up. And your lives become unlivable. What is the point of this? They're ludicrously short anyway.

Here's a thought: what if your skin is not where you end? What if you accepted that you are all that surrounds your skin? And that all that surrounds your skin is part of you?

OK, basically this: that your little stub of identity is just that, a stub, and you really shouldn't be trying to compensate with grand projects.

But you do the opposite. I really don't get it—and not in some sort of marvelling at your complexity way. No, I just think it is stupid.

Unless. Wait. Oh no, it's even worse than I thought. You just want to be immortal, little dears. You just want eternity to fall in love with you, and so you go from being demigods (of the delusional type) to fully-ballooned gods. OK, I suppose it makes sense: what else is left for you anyway? Every single one of you, inevitably and without exception, will lose everything you think you are and have when you die.

You move from diffusion to density to diffusion again so quickly that you kind of need to be pinched hard to realise that your molecules—well, my molecules—have now taken a shape that is able to understand its own finitude.

So is that what your life is? A hard pinch and then you vanish? Not entirely, you'll be glad to know. The hard pinch is your problem, so you need to decide what you want to do with it.

But vanish you don't.
You become me.
You turn into space and time folded in a measureless community of atoms.

You might not know when or where your body ends, but it's more fun that way.

## fourteen

Last night we attended our first funeral. A colleague from work died, a friend with whom we lost touch after the usual work structures broke down. We wouldn't normally have heard about it. Communications had become much more localised and old bonds had come loose, burdened by distance and the general lethargy that had invaded the city.

Exceptionally, though, we found out about it through Luz, a common friend and one of the few people who resisted the widespread tendency to recoil from traditional social engagements—she instead rode a small dinghy and flitted through the waterways as if nothing had changed. She paid us frequent but brief visits, and we couldn't help thinking that she always carried the air of an inspector checking that everything was still OK, still functioning. And we always did make an effort when we were expecting her, tidying up the flat and ourselves. She was very attuned to anything that resembled resignation to the new liquid reality and tried strenuously to get us to do things, to attend whatever concerts were happening, to join various social groups and organise initiatives about all sorts of things. We did follow her in a handful of these endeavours—in some more willingly than others, especially the ones that promised to organise us in some way so that we could defend ourselves against the general downfall. But they all seemed to fizzle out without ever getting to the second meeting, when finally action would be taken.

Despite that, Luz was indefatigable and her enthusiasm effortlessly infectious. Except for that day, when she came round to announce our mutual friend's death. We had already wiped the windows clean of their usual mist and even dried out the balcony, arranging a semblance of comfortable dryness that at that time tended to pass for hospitality. Yet, soon as she walked in, small puddles formed right where she stepped, gathering into a shallow pond of green water at the feet of the armchair when she finally sat down. We politely ignored it and tried to engage her in the usual badinage, but she blurted out almost immediately that Joe died. She called it "a perfectly normal death", somehow connected to heart failure. What she meant was that there was nothing liquid about it, nothing that came from or returned to the water, which seemed to be the source of all recent events. And for the first time since the waters, we detected in her a melancholy, a familiar ennui, a passing scent of reeds, perhaps the lapping fatigue that comes after a long period of resistance to something measureless that has been systematically flooding you from within. Far from succeeding in showing that life (and death) carried on as usual, Joe's death, in all its normality, only managed to drive home the fact that everything had changed and that neither life nor death could any longer be thought of as before the waters. Like all other failed attempts to prove that normality did carry on, this 'perfectly normal' death was, in the new circumstances, anything but normal. Even if death could, in exceptional cases, still be perfectly normal, the way death would be experienced by the city would have to be according to the new aquatic normal.

The funeral was held in a church at the other end of the city centre. As far as we knew Joe was not religious, so we suspected that the choice of location was guided by a desire to retain the old structures, or even to return to the ones that, before the waters, one used to snub. It was obvious that his family was still wealthy, whatever that meant at the time, because send-offs were usually rushed affairs that involved pushing the dead into the water and hoping for a quick wave to take them away. With most friendships and family relations in a state of collapse—unless they were aided by short distances between homes—send-offs were often left to neighbours who might or might not have known the dead.

The only way to reach the funeral spot was by boat. Luz was waiting for us on the makeshift mooring of the building next door, since ours did not have one yet. We balanced inexpertly on the gangways that arched across the windows between the buildings. While treading on these shaky pieces of already-rotting wood, we commented once again that we did not venture out very often. Our confinement was not a conscious choice, but nor did it seem an imposition. We rather felt that the liquid labyrinth around us was merely an extension of our own wet dreams of a uterine life. This is why, when safe in Luz's dinghy, wrapped in the soft dusk, undisturbed by the usual city lights, and surrounded by the submerged urban landscape that seemed to rest gently on the waterline, we could barely take our eyes off the wavelets lapping onto the moss-covered facades, and only out of politeness did we make an effort to follow Luz's renewed desire for communication, gossip, and rousing ideas about solidarity. The only things lighting the darkness were the occasional lamps left on in shops across the lower floors and their timorous reflections on the surface below—like pieces of the moon that had rained on the city and learned how to float. We crossed aquatic avenues—narrowly avoiding protruding electricity poles and still-standing traffic lights—broad boulevards whose treetops adorned the edges of the water like floating colonies of seaweed, and tight shortcuts where we could touch the rails of old balconies and walled-up windows. The water that night was sleek and black and smelled intensely of sweet rot, like a slow invitation.

When we reached the church, it was already dark. The funeral was taking place on some floating platforms forming a large circle in the space between the bell tower that was piercing the dark surface of the water like a leaning buoy, and the church's dome—a deep green-gold roundness awash with mounds of seaweed and driftwood. We moored at the back side of the dome and walked along the planks that traced its periphery right above the water surface, precariously balancing on the swell caused by other approaching boats. The space between the dome and the tower was usually taken over by kids sliding and diving into the water below, Luz told us, an improvised waterland only notionally separated from the vast urban lagoon. Last night, however, the platforms circumscribing the intimate opening of water in the middle had been decked out with icons in gilded scalloped frames, marble statues, and glimmering candelabra, all salvaged from the old church and presumably stored somewhere dry. This incongruous hall of mirrors was reflected on the surface of the dome, lending it a kind of transparency, as if the gilding, flames, and marble were not floating outside but were ensconced inside the dome's curve: all lit, golden warm, and dry. Another platform, somewhat higher than the rest and extending from a hatch opening on the dome, hosted the family, the priest, and the body tucked in a coffin.

We gathered on the various platforms, with some of us in unmoored boats grouped in concentric circles around the platform ring: friends, colleagues, family, passing residents of the city eager to witness how even the most traditional of rituals had changed. We formed an iridescent halo on the dark water surface, separated by a pool that was now almost totally still and flat, traversed only by the reflection of the bell tower, its tip almost reaching out for the dome. Everyone there had come to mourn Joe. But perhaps more than Joe; we were looking for a space to mourn our own dead, to mourn multiple unnoticed departures and sinking disappearances, friends and enemies turned into air bubbles bursting soundlessly in the folds of the waters. Everyone there brought along their own deaths: the deaths of our friends and families, of our own old selves, and perhaps above all, the death of our city and our proud verticality. We all trailed these behind us like loose ribbon ends trailing off departing boats.

But mourning was not coming easily. Everyone around us, even the immediate family, looked numb. Our emotions felt dampened by so much death so liberally spread. This was a different violence, softer but more insidious than the usual violence of survival, and it had already found its way under our skin. Apathy and, at the same time, a desire for the spectacle of death were becoming as unquestionable as the waters.

The service was brief, with the sound of singing multiplied across the water and rising in an aural whirlwind above the ring of the platforms. The dispatch, apparently aided by weights hidden in the coffin, was a soundless plunging into the pool in front of us and down the leagues of liquid vertigo that rushed along the old church facade, a sinking down into the decomposing and recomposing volumes of water. A last initiation was taking place: a body dipped in the waters of the planet's baptismal font returning to its dissolved state. The water has become our new tellurian collective, rushing in and taking over from the earth to which bodies used to return, beckoning us again to those liminal first steps. But this time in the other direction: this time, we were all walking deeper into the liquid.

## fifteen

*Long before the waters.*

I remember that misty day, several dry years ago when the air was so humid it was as if the raindrops had given up their fall and stayed suspended mid-air. I was walking in the corridor between the living room and the kitchen. I was going to get a quick drink of water or perhaps even tea and a biscuit and then carry on working. Work was quite demanding in those days and I often found myself walking in a bit of a daze, just thinking about the emails I still had to answer. I wasn't usually paying attention to where I was walking. My body would just follow the usual paths, living room-kitchen and back, living room-bathroom and back.

It took me a while to realise that I had been walking for a while and that I still hadn't reached the kitchen. I stopped for a moment, grappling with my confusion. I resumed my steps, but slower this time, counting every step. Nothing changed. The kitchen door ajar, light coming through it, was still where it had been when I had started walking. I touched the walls, spread my arms, and placed myself right in the middle of the corridor, narrow as it was, both hands touching the walls on either side. I needed to ground myself firmly in the centre of the corridor, long and vanishing into the edge of the world. There was nothing else to do but carry on walking; forwards or backwards, it didn't make any difference. The corridor had become an engorged space of your absence, continental winds blowing through it and making my body the only pivot around which the globe was turning. You were gone.

We all die small deaths every day. You had dealt with mine just as I had dealt with yours at various points in our relationship. But that one death of yours was too much. I had previously felt satisfied with myself and my ability to deal with such microemergencies. I had always followed what each time I thought you might have wanted me to do after you died. And every time had been different: I would be mourning, enclosed in an aquarium, surrounded by a wetness that would melt my skin; or I would jump out in defiance, be sociable, try to think of your glowing; or I would even take that long trip, alone on the riverboat, having to negotiate the weirs without you, relying on the presence and camaraderie of passersby, just to drop, bit by bit along the canal, all your liquidity in slow, round, silvery drops. Because that's what you wanted. Your wishes would guide me unthinkingly towards the world you wanted me to inhabit after your death. And, however hard, it was always a good world. And we would then always start anew.

But this time, I had no idea what to do, what you would wish for, what kind of world that was. I only knew that the echo was ear-splitting, and that there were no corners in which to hide from the vastness. I could see that my body was being horizontalised, spread as thinly as a forgotten caress on the earth's skin, taut from the need to deal with the immensity. In that diluted state, a thought started to emerge, as if from prehistory, attacking me like a meat tenderiser: what if this was the death of death? What if there was no more void into which to bend my body? What if this dryness was a death unto death, a double death that, instead of cancelling out death, deepened it and bloated it and made it all there was and is?

My body now felt dry and brittle, thinner than the layer of dust that remains even after a thorough vacuuming. It was as if it covered the corridor in its entirety, barely perceptible, barely there. My thoughts could no longer hold my particles together and even the slightest breeze would have torn me apart.

This time it was deeper than the previous times. And then I realised: this wasn't your death after all. It was my death. Did you know what I wanted from you? Had I told you? I couldn't remember. I was too faint to think, I had gone too deep, my brain was not responsive, my parched mouth was still gathering drops of water from wherever it could. I called you, but not by your name. My body opened up and conjured you up by your properties: your perseverance, your way of staying with me no matter what, your constancy, your density, your understanding, your elasticity, your way of connecting, your way of becoming me, your way of becoming other, your wetness, your roundness, your tense body when lying on the arch of our lives. I called the water in you.

And you heard me.

Something started softening across that dry globe of ours. Zoom in to that dappled part of a desert and listen to how it starts ever so slowly pulping up, its valley curling with the sudden pleasure that flows from otherness. And then, all those little things progressively growing to a roaring crescendo: a fleeting layer of saliva on a boy's upper lip, see how it floats away, see how it connects and becomes a drop on a dog's tail, and then tropical moisture summoned from the air around, some of it gone, some of it gathered in a half-empty glass of water, mixed with effluent from the nearby power plant; now zoom in on the crack of an old aquarium, water spilled on the floor, same but different water now, a jellyfish thrown on the beach and revived by a wave, a cloud of promise, a fist separating the surface of a lake, the same hand minutes later wiping off sweat from your forehead, and then finally your hand wiping off the dryness of my death, you: another planet as blue and jelly-like as this one, opening up your mouth and pouring out into me a stream of presence.

I came to. You were there, holding me, again and again. In our love story, both you and I are sleeping beauties, tirelessly switching places and testing each other's deaths with ever so lightly moist pecks.

# waterspeak

Was that a summons?

Not the usual god-help-me summons. White noise rubbish.

No. A vibration from within, a sort of memory.
A disembodied ripple.

I heard them.

I didn't hear any of the usual rustling, human birth and death and the little moments in between, those funny little noises emitted for a snap of a nano-second when bodies rub against the fabric of the world.

I heard their quietude.

A shared quietude, a trail of understanding noise-lessly stretching between their two bodies and across what you consider the final frontier. They didn't seem to be afraid of it or to avoid it as usual. They seemed, I don't know, to play with it. None of all the usual 'death is the end of it all', 'après moi le déluge', 'if a tree falls in a forest and no one is around to hear it, does it make a sound?', what id-iocy, yeah, babyboy, life doesn't end with you—quite the opposite, in some cases it actually begins when your end, après vous, it breathes a little breath, phew no more humans, no more of that shiny stain on the blue of my skin.

But I am getting ahead of myself—this is the future. And they are not there yet.

So, I heard this ability to reach across.
A buoyancy, a softness, a circularity.

I felt their connection to each other like a caress meant for my surfaces.

They invite me in. Their liquidity seems to flood the contours of their bodies—as if it manages to fill the space between them, making them a continuum amidst the usual human ruptures.

They called upon me when I was at my least concentrated and intense.

There are days when I am everywhere in your cities, a kind of mist or an air filled with water, floating globules you can almost taste—not talking about rain here, nor mere humidity. No, it is when I am almost there, almost visible, almost felt, almost umbrella-type of weather, almost almost.

That's one of my most exposed moments, spread thinly yet touching everything, wet to the point of saturation yet barely making the streets glisten.

It's also one of my most cherished moments, when I allow the air to tickle me and make me lightheaded. Just a bit of fun, don't judge me.

It was at one of those moments that they got me, caught my breath and stretched it across, and I had no choice but to play along.

I have no idea how they managed that.
I am obviously not romanticising anything here.
I remain perfectly aware that you all are temporary apparitions, random formulations of my body.

Yeah. But, boom, I heard them.

## sixteen

The irony of all this water but nothing to drink became painful when the city's taps stopped running.
We all knew it would happen, but somehow we still
hoped that, since there was so much water around,
we would never get thirsty. But the ability to drink
directly from the vast urban reservoir seemed re-
served for those who no longer needed it: the inverted climbers, the gill-people, the ones who spent
more time below than above the surface in some sort
of anaerobic suspension, a close-knit community of
monads who avoided contact with all of us who insisted on living on dry verticality. We all wanted to meet
someone from that fantasy tribe, ask them how they
did it, allow ourselves to be convinced to float among
the ones who never experienced thirst.

There were certainly some of us who dived. Lorna
carried on her somnambulistic underwater pursuits
long after she had exhausted the plant stock in her
former supermarket—but even she wasn't one of
them, nor had she ever encountered any, despite her
avowed eagerness to do so. We were all still bound
by our choice to carry on resisting, to always crave
the water but ultimately remain unable to embrace it
fully. And so we suffered the fate of castaways.

Our building followed the example of most other
still-inhabited buildings: we set up a rooftop reservoir that collected the rainwater and then filtered it
to a drinking tap. Around that tap we would regularly meet. Selina was often there, making new friends
and introducing people to each other as if it were a
drinks party. She had even set up a little table with
a couple of chairs where she would sit and chat with
whoever cared to linger, happy to be lifted out of
her scribbling on what seemed like an endless stock
of crossword puzzle magazines. Lorna and Marek
were rarer visitors, and when they did come up, they

always preferred to stay a bit apart from the rest of us. They were always polite and smiling, nodding at us with evident pleasure, but also moving to the other side of the rooftop, which overlooked what used to be the northern suburbs. They would stand there, briefly but with a prohibiting intensity, gazing towards the horizon and drinking in breaths of a different air, less humid and green than the mossy air downstairs at the shop. Sometimes, we would meet people we had never seen before—friends that stayed the night or the week, people in transit to somewhere else who had found temporary accommodation at our building, or once even a group of people from a different neighbourhood altogether who were doing the rounds, checking potential buildings to move into. Those ones we never saw again.

We would go up to the roof whenever we needed to, and occasionally without any real need for fresh water but just to check things out. We were all re-enacting a ritual of village life wherein news was exchanged near the main square fountain. Except that here the exchange was taking place atop a relic of a previous life: atop the progressively abandoned and precariously balancing ruins of wealth, power, and human exceptionalism. All this had been brought to its knees in a planetary pool of liquid inevitability.

Yet the rooftop afforded us a moment of illusion, allowing the water for once to recede from constant view, giving priority to the other buildings, to what used to be the neighbourhood: the much desired glass-panelled lofts, the ample terraces of the higher floors. We would often indulge this illusion that the waters had never happened and that life was carrying on unchanged. We only needed to train our eyes to ignore the obvious signs of abandon on the buildings around us, or our noses to disguise the constant smell of wet rot and stagnant undergrowth, and we were almost there, having a hot shower, calling friends, going shopping, getting ready for the evening. We knew that the descent would be much harder, that the pitiful quantities of water we took back to our flats would never allow us to carry on breathing in that illusion, but we couldn't resist it: our deluded belief that we could continue climbing our verticality as it continued to pierce the water was keeping us, we felt, alive.

## seventeen

*A few years before the waters.*

We eventually moved in together. Our domesticity was blended with intense desire, an intimacy that surprised us, a first-date nervousness that never left us, and a strangely familiar bickering that had settled in between us, initially as a joke but then quite routinely, as if we had turned into our parents and their decades of tired but fast togetherness. We bickered about many things, but one thing got to me more frequently than anything else: you never locked the door during the night. I could never tell whether you forgot, as you said, or if you were simply trying to prove a point about safety or openness or something. I always had to make sure that I locked before going to bed, even if you were the last one to come back to the flat.

My reasons were quite specific: not so much to keep the world out but to keep our water in, to stop it from running out and mixing with the water outside. Oh yes, water had already established itself in our life, and by now it had become an integral part of our domesticity, a little playful pet that followed us in every room. In fact, we had become rather possessive of our water—our very own water. We still entertained the idea, however tenuous, that our water was special, more limpid, a brighter emerald than any other water. We had the illusion that our water knew us, that it was part of us. We liked to think that our whole love affair and our subsequent relationship was lovingly mediated by this gentle, domesticated water of ours.

Yet, some evenings, when we were indulging in the mindless pleasures readily available during those dry times, such as watching some silly reality show on TV, I'm sure that we were both sharing the same lurking suspicion that perhaps our water wasn't that special after all. We never talked about this. In fact, though I cannot know that it isn't just me, I really could swear that, at those moments—when our feet were idly plodding on the surface, toes flirting with each other's or with the legs of the sofa and the moss-like carpet saturated with our familiar, domesticated water—your eyes would open up to a different world, a world outside where saints and demons might have mixed differently and where your presence would have been like a red round hot collateral ready to shriek away in pleasure.

But I never asked you, and now it's too late.

What would the point be anyway? I often imagined—no, I actually knew; not that I'd seen it, but it was as good as that. I certainly heard it happening—anyway, it haunted my dreams sometimes, when stress from work and the constant screaming of life became unbearable and my skin crawled away from all other skins, human and planetary alike. Those nights I heard, in my dreams but with this piercingly real sound, as if the alarm clock had been morphed into the crackling sound of my dream, I heard the slurping sound of emptying water: waves rushing out from underneath our door, locked or unlocked (it didn't matter after all), a domestic kenosis, a horizontal waterfall moving from within our flat and out towards the world, ships draining their waterload (useless as it is, imported from other seas and now ready to be filled with noxious oil, slow and heavy as my dreams, mixing with other waters from other cities); and then, large swathes of water, ours or others' or no-one's, waves sliding on top of other waves but in the opposite direction, this time entering our home and slowly filling what the previous water had left behind, covering the muddy floors and drenching again the wet newspapers we left floating on the floor the previous night, even the bottom shelves of the bookcases, their books now bloated and sticky. But the sound would only be woven into the fibres of my dreaming, and when we woke up and looked around unthinkingly on our way to the toilet; everything looked the way we had left it the night before, gently filled with our water, as inviting as arms opened to the morning.

# eighteen

In time, our building changed, reflecting the larger changes around us. Quite a few of the residents we used to know had left, making visits to the rooftop tap a quieter affair where one would often find oneself alone with the surrounding city. There has been some mobility within the building. People had moved up from the lower floors, not only because of the waters but also because of the vestiges of old social divisions that maintained an unspoken system of class differentiation according to the floors—better views, clearer airs. A consequence of our new aquatic existence was a mixing of social waters: running into people we wouldn't normally run into, striking up contacts with new neighbours whose backgrounds we ignored. Selina and her family were just one example of a new movement of people who, rather than emulating the old ways and trying to fit in according to what was considered good taste, were changing the space around them to suit their own needs. Our city had always struggled with its social divisions, on the one hand trying to accommodate difference by assigning, say, social housing within private buildings, and, on the other, failing to eradicate divisions by creating this upstairs-downstairs hierarchy of floors. After the waters, these tokens of social integration became real, urged on by the new necessity for property and aided by the fact that the state had all but collapsed and that the absence of police was becoming increasingly blatant. There was no one left to impose the usual tokens of social acceptance, tolerance, and integration, all those golden cudgels of the past. In some cases, we heard of organised expulsions of entire buildings, of existing residents being thrown out by incoming ones who claimed a right that was previously available to them only in small, assuaging bites. We lived in fear of this but also somehow applauded it, eager to see how this new social experiment would develop.

At the same time, we were grateful that no such incidents had occurred in our building. All things considered, conflict was contained remarkably well. An adjudicator emerged quite naturally amongst us. Marek, because of his manifest ability to listen, became our de facto conflict solver. This was aided by his reliable presence at the garden shop, which was our other natural place of congregation apart from the rooftop tap. The arrangement worked very well. We would meet at the rooftop to chat and air our views, worries, and wishes, to share gossip, and to learn news from other buildings or sometimes even other cities—gleefully accepting everything with the same degree of thirsty credulity, grateful for any piece of news we could bring back down or share with anyone who was not there at that moment. But we would descend to Lorna and Marek's shop to discuss difficulties, seek advice on things not done properly, solve neighbourly disputes, find solutions to perceived threats from the outside. These two spots—air, breeze and fresh water on the one hand, mildew, enclosure and comfortable stagnation on the other—were the architectural reflection of our mental bipolarity. And for a time, we were comfortable with this unexamined split, wanting to live both in the air, where the freshly-filtered water was prepared for human consumption, and in the deep green where water had taken over and humans were just part of the foliage.

If Selina was unofficially presiding over the rooftop, making us all feel at ease with each other and to some extent still part of an old, dry world, Marek was our unofficial underwater guide, opening up narrow paths through the dense vegetation so that we could roll out our difficult complaints, our subterranean desires, our deepest fears. It was here that most disputes arose and also got resolved. It was amidst this watery flora that we would feel armoured against an inimical world. Marek was a good listener and an even better enabler, encouraging us all to dig deeper and to come out with whatever it was that was eating us from the inside, orchestrating the discussion in such a way that we would all inevitably come out lighter, more luminous, less haunted.

But, here is the strange thing: Marek was not playing judge, listening to the sides and then imposing his decision. Rather, he was a true symphonic conductor, organising our collective will towards the desired outcome. He listened to what we needed even when it was not spoken, even when it was only sensed, and channelled the general desire towards a decision. Although these were never Marek's individual decisions, it would nevertheless be an exaggeration to say that they were taken collectively. We would often be present in the negotiations but hidden amongst the foliage, eavesdropping on the issues as if from the opposite shore, involved but also always able to walk away, to go deeper into our jungles. A different sort of spectatorship.

If it wasn't for this tendency towards isolation and closing-in, we could have been witnessing the emergence of a social utopia, with conflict resolved, regular but dispassionate public participation guaranteed, questions of property and rights fluid and shifting according to the needs of the people involved, and individualism dissolved in the pool of this aquatic collectivity yet retaining its singularity, combined with a personal freedom of a sort we had never before experienced. Perhaps even a combination of excessive freedom, heavy empty time, and flat untrammelled space where bodies would flow without anchorage. It seemed that we were all experiencing the same sensation of tireless swimming without direction, alone but in unison, closer than ever to those who managed to emerge next to us from this sea of possibilities, molecules of the same body moving alongside each other on this vertiginous flatness. Amidst that openness, there were also tender closures, nightly insularities, habitual turns of the key in the door, and returns to what we imagined our previous, dry lives to have been: huddling in with old or new beloveds, surrogate families, and lovers of one night who etched their bodies on our watery retinas for a very long time.

## nineteen

*A few years before the waters.*

We were still exploring each other's tastes and lim-
its. We were even making a conscious, perhaps even
slightly forced, effort to develop new interests in common. A Saturday trip to a bookshop yielded several
potentially interesting books. You were turning the
pages maniacally, not just forwards, but also backwards, as if you were trying to find something you
had read but now lost. That was your way of reading—quick and nervous and then, all of a sudden, a
lull, a well of words, and you would dive in, staying
on the page for so long that one would think you had
fallen asleep. A presage of things to come no doubt.

You had just found one such page and your face was
spread over it, flushed against the edges of the book,
fingers grabbing it as if it were a steering wheel. I
was sitting opposite you, reading (different book
same author), our feet touching over the coffee table.
I started getting hungry, so I thought I should ask
what you fancied for dinner. I opened the sentence
slowly and threw it over to you, just the beginning,
clear but also quiet, so as not to interrupt your concentration. You caught it in your palm and unrav-
elled it ever so slightly, just a couple of prepositions
more, and then you stood up, sentence in hand. You
walked across the room with the words trailing behind you, reached the window, and just stood there,
looking out. It was a hot early evening, with hesitant
lights across the road, the humidity from the earlier
rain still in the air. You put the end of the sentence in
your mouth and climbed out.

I hadn't realised how humid it was, but you had. You
thrust yourself out, softly and without even a tic of
nervousness, and the air held you up: innumerable tiny
bubbles made of floating water, like a hugging mat-

tress. You did that with a soft abandon that seemed to say, let's forget about dinner, let's float unencumbered, let us be fed by what is offered—no preparation, no negotiation, let's just quietly drift. You bounced and then started drifting across, gently guiding your body away from our window, with large open arms and slow-moving legs, confident in this aquatic lift. I followed you to the window and threw myself out. Not in your pursuit so much, but perhaps hoping to catch the other end of the sentence that was trailing behind you like an invitation to play. I was too slow, however, and soon gave up. I drifted in the other direction instead, bridging the air of the city with our formation: you there, me here, and between us an unfolding sentence sliding on the surface of the humid air.

## twenty

One night, after our eventide locking, someone knocked on our door. A man we had never seen before, small suitcase in hand, asked us whether he could spend the night. We stepped back from the door hesitantly, inviting him in, partly to satisfy our curiosity and partly realising the futility of the act of locking every night. It became apparent to us then that we would always end up opening the door to anyone who knocked asking to come in, whatever the hour. In any case, our door had become so flimsy and unstable— scarcely thicker than a veil of mist—and connected us more than it separated us from the immense inside in which we all floated.

The man walked in without either entitlement or obsequiousness. He sat in the armchair, placing his unopened suitcase next to him. He told us how he would drift by in his airboat (which he had constructed himself using old ceiling fans), always slowing down when passing by our building and moving as far across the width of the waterway as possible in order to get a clearer view of the interiors of the inhabited flats and shops of the building. He felt attracted to it, but he was unable to say why. By inviting himself in, he was hoping to understand what this unqualifiable characteristic was. Or so he said. It crossed our minds that this was just something he said in order to gain access to the flat, but we didn't challenge him. We ate dinner together, potential silences filled mostly by his queries about the building—not exactly indiscreet, but quite probing. We wondered why he didn't consider moving in. We even suggested a few empty flats we knew.

He avoided giving an answer, talking instead of a place he'd seen during his travels outside the city; the ricefields, as he called them, a vast expanse of shallow lake water trapped in a valley not far from the east end of the city where potentially edible kinds of vegetation could grow. He could see a future there, he said. He did seem confident about his practical skills, and he alluded in technical terms to building possibilities, to stilts and floating platforms as housing options, to cities that would explore a new verticality at peace with the flatness around them, if that's what we wanted and needed. This last sentence he delivered while getting up, leaving the table and looking at the balcony window that we could no longer open because of the humidity, or perhaps because of some other mechanical problem with which we never bothered ourselves. After offhandedly asking for our permission, and before we even granted it, he reached for his suitcase, searched for a small piece of sandpaper, and started smoothing the side of the window. Hammer, screwdriver, and then pliers followed, all while we were cleaning up the table and getting ready for sleep. We offered to set for him the bed in the study but he refused, opting for the sofa instead. Appreciatively, although somewhat mystified, we let him carry on with his work on the window and went to bed.

The following morning, we both woke up eager to find out more about the ricefields. The way he described them was strangely familiar, drawn as if from the depths of sleep not a dream but a body posture, an inclination of the upper body and a tension in the arms, or a sentence that we have read and then forgotten but whose aftertaste underlines everything we have tasted since.

But of course he had already gone. We couldn't tell whether he had slept, although the window was fixed. On the dining table, right where he sat the previous night, he had left a peculiar gift: a rectangular plastic box, transparent, filled halfway with a water so dark and murky it could have been crude oil. The box could not be prised open without breaking it. We took to playing with it after that night, idly tossing it between our fingers, feeling the frothy weight of the slow-moving mass inside, safe in its enclosure, unspilling, sullied, forever contained. In time we saw some of our neighbours bringing similar boxes out of their pockets and playing with them absent-mindedly.

# waterspeak

Look at me, all undignified, yielding to the stupidity of my involuntary anthropomorphisation.

I am becoming ever so slightly obsessed with them. You can tell, right?

Well, perhaps I am becoming human.

I don't really mean this. Not even as a remote possibility, not even as a joke.

So, these two. They are in me and yet different from me.

I now know, I am beginning to remember, I have heard them before. They were this discontinuous vibration coming from somewhere that felt remote and yet intimate, pulsing from the far end of my shorelines, from another universe perhaps, or the same universe but folded deeper into itself.

I now know. It is because they are summoning the whole of me, and they are doing it with the whole of their bodies. Not just creative thoughts about water or wavy symbols or little wet gods or even nice cooling plunges in actual watery me.

No, they have actually invited me in as a whole, dirty laundry and all. They are inviting me in with every inch of their body and at every moment.

They became water themselves, their limbs aquified.

I even became small to hear them properly. Tiny me, a bulbous reduction, my entire largesse squeezed into such things as humidity lighter than air, rain so soft that your skin does not even register it, an imperceptible film of sweat that dries as soon as it ekes out of your pores.

I did not even mind shutting myself up in demeaningly transparent bottles, stinky airtight boxes, or even rotting metal tubes this time.

And I was actually amazed it worked.

Can my universe really discern a single body?
Can my time slow down to the level of your anguishing measurings?
Can my space fold into itself so that a little incident on a beach or a discussion in a crumbling humid flat can be on a par with the spread of galaxies and the echo of black holes?

I would have said, no, no way, I would have laughed—no, actually, before hearing these two I would not even have understood those questions.

But now, yeah, of course, it makes sense. No biggie. It's like discovering an itchy little spot that you never knew you had. Tiny and indifferent up until now, but sizeable and more exigent now that it is itching you. Still part of you, always part of you, but now elsewhere; still part of you but also separate in a way.

This is what these two are to me.

## twenty-one

*A year before the waters.*

We had discovered the importance of water in containers long before the waters. We knew we should expect something from the box left on the table by our guest, but didn't know what. No rush though. We felt comfortable putting it aside and waiting for when it emerged, a message in a bottle finally reaching shore.

On the seventh year of our relationship, we decided to go for couples' therapy. Our sessions were difficult. You hardly talked. You seemed to want to keep the sessions dipped in that nervous, irritable silence, castigating me when I tried to talk about anything other than your very silence.

We had some serious issues to deal with, which we had summed up as 'the Positano incident': my rushed departure, after an unexpected invite by a friend, to Positano a few months ago had brought about several arguments, with resentment piling-up at every mention of my abandoning you for a week and your inability to understand why I had felt I had to do it. I brought you back a bottle filled with that craggy, inconvenient sea that laps the coasts around Positano, but you put it aside and didn't look at it again. We had reached a dead end, our discourse a knot whose ends were lost deep in our testiness.

Yet something was still salvageable. In our different ways, we both tried. We had acquired the habit of going to a small restaurant for dinner right after the weekly sessions, carrying with us the frustration and anger that inevitably surged during the therapy hour, but also united in ridiculing our therapist, finding fault with everything from dress sense to way of sitting—upright and primly waiting for us, or rather you, to talk. We ended up prizing those dinners together even more than the actual therapy. At those moments, we could both see plainly that we were not on opposite camps, that we really did want to untangle our difficulties.

But the most decisive moment came from you. One evening, after a couple of months in therapy, at our usual table at the restaurant, you opened your bag and fished out the bottle I brought you from Positano. I did not recognise it right away—I had forgotten about it, and anyway it looked like any bottle of water. You placed it on the table, between us but without it blocking our view of each other. You asked me whether I wanted a taste. I looked at you bemused but also amused; a new game, let's do it, whatever might come out. You opened it and poured some into my wine glass. You did this from a slight distance, so that the water billowed forth from the bottle, splashing and swirling vigorously.

And then it stopped. The swirl of the water froze, or did we freeze, witnesses to an elastic time that was swallowing us up? The water appeared like a mini ice sculpture, perfectly nested within the walls of the glass, round yet undulant, its edge nosing up from the glass edge and turning into an elegant Japanese-looking curl. We looked at that moment and its duration, seemingly infinite and drawn out, no end in sight. We looked at that space, open, connected: on the one side, English rain falling soft on our uncovered heads; and, on the other, eddying waves sparkling under the late summer Italian sun. We were granted an unexpected infinity, and we walked in, hand in hand, in awe of how time and space could fan out so much that we could be swallowed by one single event. The Positano incident, horrifically long, blissfully long, the same event this and that side, its duration a stretched blank canvas. We touched the wave with our fingers and tasted it, fresh as return, ancient as departure.

Maturity: when the open finally opens around us, and our love for each other does not block the view.

## twenty-two

After the first wash, when the whole city stank unbearably for weeks, things settled to a continuous undertone of mild rot and humidity, redolent of wafts creeping out of a rarely-visited basement. We got used to it and hardly ever noticed, except on certain days during the summer months when the water seemed to boil, ejecting from its open watery wounds its undigested histories.

Our sense of smell changed too, perhaps as a defence. It became blunt and impervious to the daily changes, the minutiae of our watery existence, treating them as a background to living. At the same time, though, it also became keener, sniffing out odours from a much greater distance than we were used to. Cooking and other domestic smells had been reduced, so we really sat up and sniffed when cardamom-strong curry pots were being prepared by a family a couple of buildings downstream, or when anything other than fish and bird was being roasted anywhere in the vicinity. Animal smells were confined to those buildings that had been taken over by surviving street dogs and cats—domestic pets now being all but extinct. Rats were abundant, and their odour had joined that of the water in a melee of oversweet, swampy constant.

The water sharpened our olfactory sense in some rather unexpected ways. People often talked about how they knew if the neighbours were unwell, or if the people along the corridors were sad or even more closed-in and isolated than usual. At building gatherings, people would be preceded by a sort of olfactory aura that allowed us to know not only who was coming from around the corner but also, as they got closer, how they were feeling on that day, whether they were angry, sad, happy, or resigned. But this awareness was not the result of a rational analysis—'she smells like this, therefore she must be happy'. Rather, it was all done on a pre-conscious level where the other's fears and desires would emerge within us, as if from an inner fold of our own body, notionally connected to the other person. It was as if—and this was often the best way to talk about it—a subaquatic synchronisation was taking place wherein our saliva, sweat, pus, all our incandescent ponds of body fluids, would tremble with a knowledge both ours and yet never fully ours.

Our liquid inner worlds would ebb and rise in some sort of communicative inland waters, communicating not just with people but increasingly with the surviving animals of the city, the passing seagull, the new kinds of fish and reptiles that had colonised what used to be streets and shops and offices, and even the plants that burst from the waterline below or took over lower floors and balconies across the city. We would often find ourselves on a non-linguistic continuum with everything else, unable to express what it was that we were feeling but ultimately drenched in an all-enfolding awareness of the submerged city's mood, an awareness so intense and saturating that we had neither the means nor the desire to escape, delving deeper into it with every syncopated breath.

# twenty-three

*The year before the waters.*

We were very unlucky with our fish. We used to call it the death trap, that glass box of a grave that managed to kill off whatever fish we introduced into it. We had tried hard, experimenting with different kinds of fish, varying water temperatures, plants and no plants, minimal and over-the-top kitsch decoration.

After several attempts, several upturned deaths, and as many summary toilet send-offs, we realised that the only things doing reasonably well were the water plants. So the aquarium became a sort of flooded terrarium, a mini earth abandoned by its fauna, its bottom covered in white pebbles, the oxygen machine still gurgling up its bubbles—mainly for the aesthetics of it, since we did not know whether it made any positive difference to the plant life. And the plants had free reign, taking over the space undisturbed by fish, rotting food flakes, or our maladroit attempts at cleaning the aquarium, medicating the water, or changing the decorations in the hope that some fish would survive.

In time, pebbles and glass walls started turning mossy green, as if the plants were extending their chlorophyllic tentacles in an attempt to shield themselves from our gaze. The aquarium steadily became murkier and dirtier, much more so than when we had fish. This monospecies expansion seemed to be devouring the outside world, enclosing itself in a cloudy, green, impenetrable bubble. We did not intervene except for adding water to replace what had evaporated. During one of these operations, which were somewhat delicate because of the need to keep the glass lid open with one hand while pouring from a fairly heavy jug with the other, you carelessly managed to cut your arm on the glass, dropping the jug in the tank and splashing the walls around it with thick green water. The red spread against the green, a strip of an island across the ocean.

I came over, as if attracted to the smell, and stood there looking. You had to nudge me, bring some paper towels! Come on, help a little! I went to the kitchen while you were trying to pick up the jug from the tank. I rushed back but brought no paper. I have an idea, I said. I took your arm with the already pulsing red wound and gently introduced it into the aquarium, holding it immersed, a red line trailing off it and swirling around the plants. You trusted me, and I wanted you to trust me, although I was not sure why I was doing this. I held your arm there, speaking to you all along, trying to calm your worries about wound infection and presenting this patently absurd idea as the right thing to do. You jerked your arm out, clearly unconvinced, splashing even more water all around, and in the process jerking me out of my almost somnambulistic state. I rushed to the kitchen, brought paper towels and plasters, and in short did what was expected of me, feeling sorry for my earlier lapse and tending to your wound with inflated attention.

The following morning, you woke up earlier than I did. I laid in bed, thoughts of remorse mingling with worry about actual infection and a certain anxiety about our relationship. I still had no idea why I had held your arm in the water. Part of me genuinely felt that it would help. Another, deeper and murkier part of me, however, might have wanted to hurt you—a punishment for your clumsiness, or the expression of an irritation that at that point I was not feeling but that I am sure was there somewhere. Perhaps I just wanted to see more of that red in the green. Or I was only thinking of the aquarium, and wanted to offer it something as a sacrificial apology for all the pains we had caused it.

When I finally got up and walked into the living room, I saw you: arm submerged in the aquarium, wound open in this underwater jungle. It was a good idea after all, you said.

We had already started inhabiting the wet enclosures of our future.

When these two plunged their arms into me, something strange happened: I remained unaltered.

Well, some things moved inside me, but my depth
did not deepen, my volume did not increase. There
was no displacement. It was as if their bones and
tendons were already part of my volume. I did not
swell, I did not grow wider.

Almost—I don't know—almost kindly? Their arms
nudged my folds to the side, their blood drifted in my
innards, nestling somewhere inside me, causing the
softest movement. But there was enough room for all
of us. There was no need for me to escape the aquarium, to spill over, or to raise my surface even a little.

We fused together, them and me. Whatever boundaries there used to be, they have now dissolved. My
molecules on either side of their skin joined up.

A continuum.

It takes a wound to make us flow together.

Perhaps. I don't know. I am learning. Am I? How
can I learn, if there is nothing outside me? How
can I change, if I am time? How do I come closer to
anything, if I am distance? How do I give death, if I
am life?

Just to clarify things, I don't like these two very
much. I mean, I am interested in them, but it is not
a question of liking them or not. I can still be objec-
tive, even though for my standards I realise I must
sound utterly besotted.

But so what? Acting paradoxically is my prerogative.
Anyway, I don't really like these two. In fact,

I am getting angry at their unquestioning self-indulgence, their slow apathy, their maddening solipsism.

Not that I am interested in some sort of human morality, but, gosh; it's all about connecting to the bodies around you, isn't it. It's all about linking up, forming common fronts—and they are really bad at it.

OK they are kind of trying, but so listlessly that it's a joke. They seem to be sporting the worst elements of their species.

I sometimes think they are even worse than the others. Bad neighbours and bad citizens, bad friends and bad lovers, they are just worried about their own little selves, indifferent to what their own species is inflicting on their planet and on me in particular. They disgust me; I am so repulsed by them I tremble!

And yet.

They link with me. They flow along with me. I mean, not fully. Not nearly there. But there is promise.

They open something in me so old that it is beyond time. They might be opening me up to my own self, making me see my multiplicity, my extremes, even my paradoxes.

Oh I am furious.

## twenty-four

Flattened by pools of horizontality and almost blasé about water, we had forgotten what a deluge might feel like. We were forcefully reminded of it one night, when the sky, a dull bowl cupped over the city dim with a diffused luminescence borrowed from what seemed like a different epoch, started liquifying, a huge pool of water suspended for a minute as if surprised at the sight of its own reflection on the submerged city below, dallying in its aerial narcissism for just a moment longer, and then collapsing, a viscous blanket thrown over the whole urban sprawl, a single stentorian bang rising at the exact same moment from all the neighbourhoods across the city, rapping on every water surface and facade, not in drops or sheets of rain but in compact opalescent volumes, hard aquifers colliding with the city water and breaking it, converting its usual spreading softness into a brittle panic, our city water now unable to withstand or even gracefully accommodate this invasion, water but different, not of the city, massive pillars of diluvial ferocity that were effortlessly wedged into and displacing our painstakingly amassed aquatic reality, not even pretending to be one of us but rather a water that was screaming its incongruity, as if taking pleasure in this frontal attack, inebriated by its own force and the ease with which it breached our defences, gleefully savouring the feebleness with which our city fell to the flood.

## twenty-five

*The year before the waters.*

A Sunday sun always meant trying to convince you to go for a long drive out of the city—yes, it now sounds inconceivable that at the time we used to be able to leave the city. What would now be a gift, perhaps the ultimate gift, was at the time a moot point between us. Your ideal Sunday always involved staying in, flicking through random TV films, passionately identifying with the various characters for five minutes and then moving on to the next film. I admit that I often enjoyed that too. But when the sun is pouring in, my whole body starts to push me out, and wants you along. So, one day, after a little egging, we started.

We lightly packed the new hamper you had bought me for my birthday—crackers and cheese, some fruit, chocolate, and a bottle of wine—and off we went. I was driving, blinded by Sunday melancholy, the sun in my eyes and a breeze coming in from the window, the smells of the city slowly giving way to iconic scents of supposed freedom or weekend family fun. You see, I was aware of how we were, at that very moment and at other moments like it, embodying an urban cliché, a sense of freedom constructed on the back of a life consumed in immunity, relative shade, and ill-fitting velocity. I was aware of how that drive was merely a way to perpetuate another week of no-picnic, of no-aimless driving or illusion of freedom, and perhaps because of this awareness—or perhaps because I was following the sun instead of the GPS, or perhaps even because I followed a different desire altogether—I drove us to the other side of the day: that pool of green-blue dusk that spreads around midday where I used to dip my feet when I was little, that dark slice of the day that I had often folded around me when I was taking a nap.

You did not notice.

It was still quite bright anyway, and we were chatting away. At some point the playlist shifted to a piece of music at odds with the rest, one that had been randomly included who knows how, and that made you notice. You asked me where I was driving to. I felt the need to pretend that we were still heading to our planned destination. A part of me actually still thought we were, that nothing had changed—just a few clouds and that was it. You were not convinced, of course, but you said nothing more. We kept on driving, circling the lake shore. I had to switch on the night lights, and I did so with a certain trepidation. I felt that this would be the decisive point when you would say, enough now, let's turn back. But you didn't. And we carried on in a sweaty complicity. The road around the lake was narrow and empty, although we did encounter a few other cars, mostly coming from the opposite direction. But a circular road being just that, circular, all directions seemed to be leading back into the circle.

We drove non-stop for what felt like years—perhaps it actually was years and not just a few hours. It was an inordinate amount of time anyway, as if our whole relationship had been unfolding on that narrow lane by the lake, dipped in a perpetual dusk, with us occasionally chatting but mostly relying on the playlist's loop. The lake was much larger than I remembered. I had in mind a small pool of dark fluorescent light with a barely trodden track around it. When you revisit your childhood places, you usually find them smaller, narrower, shallower—in short, lesser. This was exactly the opposite: the vastness of the lake spreading before me had overtaken my adulthood, swamping it with the inexorable trickle of an hourglass I had forgotten all about until I suddenly realised that it had run out.

We stopped the car and stepped out. The silence was thick and powdery. I picked up the hamper from the back seat, a last gesture of normality. Everything was dusk-dark, with freshly ground Prussian blue sprinkled over the pebbles and the plants surrounding the lake. The only light that evening was coming from the lake, but it was inaccessible in itself, refracting only through the globules of humidity and quiet that filled the air. I fumbled on the wet ground with my palms and then decided to sit down anyway. You stood, in the posture of someone standing where the waves break and admiring a spectacular sunset. You might have even shaded your eyes with your hand—or perhaps you were just shutting your eyes even more firmly. I could not see clearly. You then turned to me and said, there used to be a sunken town in here, right in the middle of the lake. I used to rest on its central spire when I got tired of swimming. Want to swim and try to find it? It might still be there.

At that point, sadness descended as if the lake had covered me up completely. I realised in a suddenly devastating breath that we had been talking about a completely different lake. That you might have never been to the same lake as me when we were little. That you might not have been in that car with me when I drove to this lake, leaving the day behind. You must have been in a different car, listening to a different playlist and talking about different nothings. You might have just arrived, or you might have been here for some time. I realised that, at best, you might have been in one of those cars circling the lake, driving in the opposite direction. I felt helpless. I said nothing for a little while. I then got up, walked towards you, and searched for your hand in the dark. I wasn't sure I could really do this, but I thought I had to at least try. I needed to start, once again, as if from the beginning, yet also in infinite repetition, every time anew. I needed to start getting to know your hand's skin, broken by our estranged familiarity.

And now, in this lake that covers our past, present, and future, we find ourselves always starting again, every time anew, every time lost, never finding the same sunken city again.

**twenty-six**

Our city had invited the water in.

Not just in its avenues and parks and second floors, but in its very definition. Our city was now the water. It could never be thought, contemplated, or even dreamt of without water. It was slowly but inexorably changing into a shelled existence on submerged poles made up of bourgeois dreams and still-standing civil-society arches, surrounded by the vast flatness of a pitiless reflector. We were witnessing the slow process of everything we thought we knew about the city drowning.

And not just the city. We imagined the planet—we had to imagine it, no NASA images could reach us— as a sphere consisting entirely of water, miraculously kept together in a vast dark aridness. While dreams of flying persisted, their frequency was reduced; they ceded their place to those other dreams where we practised an underwater existence, a continuous, effortless, breathless sliding, with our arms cutting the waters in thick slices.

We knew that we were experiencing the collapse of our civilisation, a sinking down of all the struc tures we held sacred, immovable, or at least in- evitable. At times these structures would emerge in conversations, sometimes nostalgically but mostly as threats. So, while the idea of the state seemed to have completely disappeared, some would bring it up as future menace, as in the example of a neigh- bouring state's appetite to invade us. Another social structure of the dry times were the then-ubiquitous multinational companies, whose usual everyday in- fluence had disappeared, leaving behind only some faded logos on billboards and building facades. Some would bring this up in discussions, inevita- bly branding them as the parties responsible for the waters. But these theories were swiftly dismissed, either because there was hardly any reason for anyone to invade anyone else, or because nobody could see how or why the multinationals would have done this, considering that nothing of what we still had could draw any interest from them, and that no one could afford to buy the products that had made them rich.

Of course people liked to lament their fate and to blame the waters—this was the usual beginning of the chats around the rooftop tap or in corridors. But these seemed like another half-hearted attempt at clinging on to a dry normality. Behind the facade of the lament lurked a resigned indulgence, a gleeful anticipation signalled by quick dismissive gestures that aimed at moving the discussion on to what was really the desired focus of most conversations: the water and its behaviour. Selina would often preside over such conversations, or certainly initiate them in the off-hand but inviting way she had of commenting on the water the way we used to comment on the weather during the dry times. This sort of aquatic gossip revolved around the appearance of the water today, its smell, movement, or temperature; or the way water would emerge in various places, in flats and through walls, in new configurations, and was that the same or different water, was it our water or was it other water, and yes, fine, mix it, but how much can we take? A new ethics of territory but this time entirely liquid, with a veneer of possessiveness that would quickly fade, ceding its place to a form of reluctant admiration for the water's unflagging ability to mingle, to undifferentiate, to become one, to flow and surge and yet remain smooth and round.

So after the initial obligatory lament, we would wax lyrical about this morning's reflections on the surface of the water below, our eulogy only momentarily marred by a passing regret. And while initially the regret was about the damages and inconvenience caused by the waters, it quickly became about our inability to become even more liquid ourselves, more of the now and less stuck in the arid nostalgia of the past.

Along with these two, I also hear their city.
No longer loud, no longer alive.

I hear its dying, low-lying gurgles and subsidence.
I hear its evanescence—madly precipitated, they did
not expect it, too fast they say, not yet, why now?
And here we go again, time stretching, we were
going to live for ever.

They still hope, climbing up on their technology
and helplessly gazing at my flat horizon. But their
crutches are sinking deeper into my silt.

I have begun to understand something that I don't
think I could have understood earlier. Also, not sure
whether understanding is what I want to say here.
Feeling, maybe—jelly-like vibrations across my
liquid bodies. OK.

So I have realised that ever since I started hearing
them, my body has occasionally become oddly restless, as if it can feel a boundary it has never
felt before.

I am not talking about silly bottles and even sillier
dams.

I am talking about big boundaries, the types that
emerge from within and that haunt one's movement.
I can hear how these two are haunted by their own
boundaries—not by the ubiquitous boundary of
their own skin or by each other's presence or that
of others around them, not even the city or me and
my obsessive eavesdropping (but I do it so elegantly,
right?). No, not these.

Or perhaps these too, but only as manifestations of
another boundary: grander, insuperable, invisible.

The more invisible it is, the more diffused it becomes in all these other little things. The more invisible it is, the more it commands their lives.

So how can I feel human death as mine? What would death mean to me?

Nothing. I mean, it would actually mean nothing.

Our nothings are of course different. These two fear death as nothing, their own little nothing (again!), their own little death (again!), 'not I anymore'—getting irritated with all this parochialism.

But what I mean is that their nothing means their own end. I obviously know otherwise: they never really end. They just become me, and they carry on with me becoming other me.

Alright, this is not a philosophy lesson, I have drowned many philosophers in my bosoms, and they too have got it all wrong—mostly, anyway.

This is just to say that their nothing is stupid, narrow-minded, typically human.

But my nothing—well! That's a whole different story. If I reach nothing, then the whole nothing reaches its nothingness; it doubles up, the end of all ends, nothing wrapped in nothing, and you know what that means! No, you don't, I am just teasing. Of course you don't.

So take my word for it: this nothing is serious. It will not just be the end of your youth, your life, your children's life, your thought, your beauty, your planet, your world. It will not just be the end of the world, or even the end of the universe.

It will be the end of end. Never another beginning. Never another never.

This makes me feel an agitation, a nervousness. A bit fragile, that's how it feels. I guess shame, too: I am expected to be omnipotent and here I am, maudlin and weepy, thinking of my death.

It's all their fault, of course. I am my own hallowed pool, and all of a sudden I feel my feet (manner of speech) dangling off the end of the water, with a dry, dark universe underneath. I suppose it's a bit like the way you feel in the sea when your feet can no longer touch the ground. And you can't swim.

Alright, it's gone now. Back to normal.

## twenty-seven

*The year before the waters.*

We tried introducing other lovers into our relationship. Sometimes these were instant fallings-in-love that one of us would invite into our world for a night or two; at other times we would succumb to some long-standing infatuation, more an intellectual attraction than pure physical desire. These lovers would tread awkwardly around our love for each other. They would sometimes claim more space than they were allocated, becoming possessive or insecure about what they were supposed to do. Others would shy away from it all, perhaps too afraid to deal with the complexity of our relationship. We felt for them, we really did, and often tried to make it easier by concealing some potentially difficult facts about ourselves. We hardly ever spoke to them about the water between us. We were certain they would not understand—how could they? We ourselves hardly did—or they would take it as some sort of eccentric but potentially inviting fetish.

Our imagination, however, always proved stronger than we thought, and our own connection to each other expanded and swallowed up the desires and resistances of our lovers. Every single one of them was eventually pushed out, even from our memory. They fleetingly united us on a common front of experimentation, only to eventually deliver us back to our amorous womb.

And yet, during this ceaseless coming and going, something was put aside, a stash of desire for another kind of permanence, a different kind to the one we shared. Throughout our relationship I kept a lover who was never to be introduced to you, a secret lover. I am sure that you did too, sure in an unverified way that had to remain unverified, however tempting it might have been to start looking around for clues. And the clues would not be particularly hidden either.

I kept mine completely transparent, in a perfectly round snowball, complete with floating flakes and even a little castle in the centre. And in yet another gesture of transparency, I did not hide the snowball but rather kept it in an easily accessible drawer, the one where we stored all those knives we never bothered sharpening. I had acquired the habit of dumping the newly blunt knives abruptly, relishing the clanking sound. I did worry a little that I might end up breaking the snowball and spilling my lover out. But I worried more that the indifference with which I used to replace our knives, and the matching hope (by now impossible to take seriously any more) that I would eventually—perhaps on a slow Sunday morning—get round to sharpening them, were a sign that something was not quite right between us, an inherent obsolescence indelibly etched into our bodies and the space between us, one that would eventually catch up with us.

Maybe this was the reason why I kept my secret lover in that drawer—not as an alternative solution in case things went bust, but as a reminder of this very obsolescence. It was my defence against what we both perceived as the inevitable end of us, a keep-me-alive otherness that tickled us even in those moments that echoed from deep within those vast future lands where there would no longer be any sharpness left between us.

When those moments were becoming more proximate than just a faraway horizon, I would open the drawer and search within it, careful not to cut my hand on the blades that, blunt as they were, were still able to hurt me, and I would roll my secret lover out. I would hold the snowball in my hand, a perfect cool roundness inviting me to shake and shake until the promised whirlwind spectacle took place. But if I resisted shaking the snowball straight away and, with ginger movements, placed it on the kitchen counter, allowing any agitation to settle, I could still discern the face and body of my secret lover just next to the little plastic castle.

But on the occasions when I took the snowball and shook it vigorously to make all these bits of glitter move about, I could see, not without a certain dull joy, that even this lover (whose skin remained the same even as everything underneath that skin seemed to change, stretch, and flatten out), yes, even this lover, subcutaneously and perhaps more hesitantly than all the others, but nonetheless without a doubt, without surprise, and without escape, was slowly turning into you.

## twenty-eight

We sometimes wondered what happened to all the great works of art that used to adorn the city, especially the collections of the city's museums and galleries. In the paralysis that followed the waters, art could hardly have been a priority. Those deep storage basements of the city's museums must have been flooded and abandoned, paintings and statues rotting in the new reality whose only art was that of surviving. But we were mistaken. We were soon to find out that there were people much more desperate than we were to maintain the illusion that nothing had changed, holding onto Renaissance paintings and twenty-first century installations as if they were rafts.

We were to discover this when Luz invited us to attend a party at the State Gallery of Art on Sunday evening, "to celebrate the beginning of the season". We didn't know the host, but Luz seemed to be fairly confident that we would be welcome. The invite was printed on hard watermarked paper, even including an RSVP which of course we had no means of honouring. Luz was vague about the arrangements and the host's name, and seemed to be as surprised as we were about the location, although she pretended otherwise. It was very important for her still to be considered a woman of the world, well-connected and *au fait* with all the cool happenings.

We waited on the usual promontory at the agreed time, dressed in clothes that we'd forgotten we had and that were utterly at odds with the risk of getting soiled by the uneven floor of the planks, or drenched by waves whenever a boat passed by. Luz had cleaned her dinghy fairly thoroughly but, even so, we managed to stain our clothes with the ubiquitous green hue coming off the mossy surfaces. The gallery was boarded up and no light could be seen anywhere, certainly nothing that would signal a gala inside. We sailed round the building a couple of times, passing under the tall stone arches that linked the central building to its wings. By now, they had been reduced to little more than eyelids leaning heavily on the water, leaving only a sliver of a passage, tall enough for small boats with crouching passengers to pass through. We were perhaps too ready to write the whole thing off as a bad joke—a memento of old times that somehow reached us now by mistake—or to ascribe the situation to a confusion about the dates or even just a late change of mind on the part of the host, when we saw the gangway perilously extending from the roof of the old gallery and leading to what seemed like an open hatch. We tried to moor there, but since there was nothing to throw our rope around, we agreed to wait on the boat while Luz walked in and checked.

She re-emerged a few minutes later, an expression of amused surprise on her face. Right behind her, a young woman was following in something that looked like a hotel uniform, black with golden details. She walked decisively towards the boat, officiously apologising for the wait. We disembarked and walked through the hatch into the gallery building, while the woman in the uniform took the boat away, presumably to moor it till we needed it again. Hardly a sound was coming through. Luz was reassured by the woman that the party was taking place as expected. We only had to reach the end of the corridor.

We went down a few steps, turned to the right, then turned again. We had been walking for a while up and down narrow staircases and long stretches, plunging deeper into a dimly lit corridor full of mossy silence, when the first sounds other than those of our steps reached us. But these were no party sounds. The closer we got to their source, the more convinced we became that we had simply walked through the interior of the whole building in some sort of ancillary service passage and that we would end up on its back side, facing the city once again. The only sound we could hear was a vigorous aquatic bubbling-up, not unlike the sound the old sewers emitted when they overflowed.

We finally arrived at the end of the corridor and entered the belly of the gallery: the grand central hall, a majestic ballroom-type room with damask silk wallpaper and dark oak panels, all loomed over by the famous grand chandelier—a sprawling Venetian affair whose tentacles seemed to extend to the whole stuccoed ceiling. Some of the collection's masterpieces were traditionally showcased in this hall, from which all other corridors and rooms fanned out, and to which everyone converged at some point during their visit. But now, instead of admitting visitors, all the corridors and adjacent rooms had turned into water avenues, tributaries to a dark inland delta. Thick volumes of water were being poured into a vast central pool that extended deep into the storage basements, a cross-section of the building filled with water. Rather than cascading, the tributaries seemed to be feeding into the pool from beneath, silently bubbling in and mixing with one another. Massive filters were fitted on every aqueduct, converting the usual brackishness into a liquid crystal as clear and nuanced as the chandelier spreading directly above it. What made the whole scene even more incongruous was the obscene quantity of masterpieces hanging floor-to-ceiling—vulgarly placed one on top of another—on every inch of the walls surrounding the giant pool, and the various Rodins, Giacomettis, and Bourgeoises placed on raised podiums and platforms scattered around the pool waters as if they were water features. And in that deep effervescence, amidst this trembling memento of outlandish luxury and this desperate harking to an imagined past, no more than a couple of handfuls of people were lounging about, swimming or perching on the sides of the pool, cocktails in hand or simply sitting on the edge, feet playfully in the clean, cool water.

This was clearly the extent of the party. The beau monde reduced to a few disperati, probably as fake and random as our presence there, unbelonging and uninterested, united only by a saturnine curiosity and perhaps a desire to pretend that all was good, and that the only water that mattered was to be found in this pool. We were confronted with ultimate luxury at its most histrionic: in the city of water, water was elevated to the ultimate commodity. There was nothing natural about this Edenic reconstruction. It was merely a folly of baroque magnitude.

The whole set-up was the abode of our host, a man who used to work in the gallery as a security guard, as we were quickly told by a talkative waiter. Our host had apparently sold a vast amount of art to whoever had the money, and with his gains he had constructed this pharaonic reproduction of the outside reality that was ensconced within the building—a sort of lab where the contingency of waters gave way to a hydraulic aesthetic control. Our host never bothered to speak to us, sitting on a Bauhaus-type chair enclosed in a glass box, a Francis Bacon pope communicating with the outside through microphones. We were told that he never used the pool—preferring instead a small transparent plastic container filled with clean water, in which he kept his feet for hours on end—and especially whenever there were guests around.

The same waiter told us that our host had printed out thousands of invitations in the gallery's print room, every batch with different dates, about two hundred for every day of the year. He was sending them to whichever addresses he could muster, randomly selected or sometimes even just made up, and when there were no more postal deliveries he recruited people who would slip the invites underneath random doors. There were never more than a couple of handfuls of people, and increasingly even fewer than that, to the point that this last week only once or twice had anyone showed up. The waiter was especially happy that tonight there was quite a buzz.

We quickly left that odd democratic experiment, where the water had to be processed in a vainglorious attempt to reconstruct a past that was clearly unable to rescue us. The uniformed woman was waiting outside, seated at the end of the plank, booted feet dangling just above the water. She was holding a rope, at the end of which was our boat. She had never bothered mooring it anywhere. Upon seeing us, she sprang up with incongruous readiness and almost saluted us in a military manner, while pulling the boat up close so that we could step in.

On the way back, once the dizzy exchange of impressions had ebbed away, a numbness descended. We felt drained by the melancholy of this barren nostalgia, more saddened than impressed by the nouveau-riche aquatic cornucopia. Nothing, not even art, could save us from this passive horizontality.

## twenty-nine

Sprays of nostalgia would often reach us and haunt our everyday. Sometimes they would take us back to the dry times, when we could think of our city and even ourselves away from water, unflooded, unreflective. Water at the time was something mostly marginal, another thing to consider, a kind of distance on a Flemish blue horizon that could make our days look deeper, or the momentary green intimacy of a canal overarched by a foot bridge. We imagined water in the dry times as nothing more than background, a taken-for-granted and easily dismissed presence.

The days when nostalgia for the dry times invaded us were heavy days: water was unbearable to us, flooding our mouths and blocking our nostrils in a repulsive embrace.

Then there was this other nostalgia, perhaps already more resigned and certainly less hurtful: the nostalgia for the early days of the waters, when we still maintained a semblance of normality, when electricity was still providing an unreliable but near constant light and the internet was still delivering news and connections. Those were the days of roof-terrace restaurants and bars, large balcony parties, municipal transport, shaky floating surfaces, new neighbours, constant movement. Those were also the days of fear of course, lest the waters rose further and swallowed up the semi-dry reality that we had constructed with so much difficulty.

Perhaps also for this reason, there was a general sense of solidarity during those times: come now, one last breath until we emerge from the depths. There was a shared feeling that we all belonged on the same side—dry, human, built-up—as opposed to the other side: vast, liquid, and menacing. We were all enlisted in the battle against this one element, postmodern

Robinson Crusoes organising our floating islands like fortresses to keep the water out, stocking up on tinned food and dry property spaces from the wreck of our ship as it lay nearby in full view. Because this city of ours was still beautiful in its verticality, even if slightly askance. Our city was still the crest of our humanity and, especially, our adaptability. We had persevered and had ultimately mastered our invader, reducing it yet again to a simple aesthetic parameter, a pretty albeit savage background to our daily doings. Those were the times of new social orders, a democracy of social form and higher building floors where people would mix with each other, pushed by curiosity and a sense of an urgent need for a solution. Those were the days—and, especially, the nights—when conflict was solved with conflict, by a drawing of lines and a violent ostracisation of whoever wasn't with us in this. Those would have also been the days of leaders, of men (usually) who would see the future and guide us towards it in more or less convincing ways.

But, luckily, we were prevented from reaching that stage. Nothing dramatic really happened that helped to swerve the flow of history, no grand events or further water rises. It just happened. Right then, at a point in history only known with precision once it had passed, when things could have gone as they usually have done in the story of humanity, with leaders promising to bring us out of our crisis speaking to the masses in seductive whispers and taking possession of our consciousness, only to plunge us into even deeper crises festering with unutterable sadness and uncontained violence; right at that point, something descended upon our precariously-organised island— an unexpected man Friday, a mist, a dust wet with otherness, a cloud of airborne globules that brought upon us a torpor so gigantic that it left none of us awake to listen to the whispers. Those were the days when we first started to close in on ourselves, our flats, and our buildings. During those diving-in hours, we came in contact with something that we ignored then but we have finally just begun to understand now: our continuum with the water.

These days, there is another nostalgia that often blurs our day vision and softens our evenings. It is a future nostalgia: a tall, sky-high, elegantly-arched bridge rising from our bodies and the currents within them that ebb and flow, and linking them with the planet as it is now, covered in smooth emeraldness, a round continent that belongs to its surface.

## thirty

*A few months before the waters.*

It was my idea to convert the guest room into a little intimacy corner for us. Fancy idea, I know, but it
could still double up as a guest room whenever needed. During the dry times, family guests and friends
from abroad were visiting regularly—a bit too regularly in fact, to the point that sometimes we just
wanted to say no. So we were going to use this as an
excuse, the guest room that was no longer mainly a
guest room. There was to be just a small bed and nice
large cushions, some books on the shelves, no TV, no
harsh lights, no mobile phones. A meditative space
that we could share, a niche where our bodies could
find each other, an island of togetherness.

While we were experimenting with it, you suggested
that we pour some water around it, a semblance of a
moat keeping our love castle safe. You started tracing
the room's perimeter with a watering can, leaving a
thin line of water around its walls. I was happy to play
along, and even suggested we lay down a small wood-
en plank as a passage from the living room into the
room, signalling a bridge that only we could cross.

In time, the room became our secret boudoir, visited regularly whenever our bodies needed each other, a room of contained violence and consented-to
tenderness. You would often enter the room first,
summoning me while waiting in some sort of mock
seductive pose—mock but effective, an invitation of
limbs and arms that hardly ever went unheeded.
Sometimes we would spend the night there, pulled
closer to each other than usual because of the narrow bed, a floating embrace caressed by the quiet
volume of water separating us from the world. We
were so lulled into this plenitude of intimacy that
we progressively stopped having sex, or even being

particularly intimate with each other, outside that room. In time, the thin line of water you had poured around the room's walls started widening and deepening. I don't know whether it was you pouring progressively more water, or whether the water was once again taking over our lives in some mysterious way. But our little floatation tank was becoming more and more surrounded by water, to the point that the little floorboard we had playfully placed as an imitation of a bridge was turning out to be shorter than needed. Not wanting to get our feet wet as we went in and out, we added an extension to it. And so it went on.

One day, thinking that I heard your voice from the room, I started walking across until I reached the further end of the extended bridge. I then stopped, took my clothes off, and dived. We stopped bothering with the woodplanks from that point onwards. It was only a short shallow swim to the room anyway. The water was generally warm and kind, the view of the room beckoning, an island of a room, its door ajar letting out a soft light that was reflected on the water surface. I particularly enjoyed that swim at dusk, when the light from outside was softer and the waters took a peach-red lustre. I lifted myself up to the door of the room (we needed to add a rail or something here because it was getting too slippery) and entered You were not there. I must have misheard. The room was empty and  felt bigger than usual, perhaps because you were not there, or rather because, even at times when you were not there at first, you always came shortly after, so that the room was already filled with the expectation of your arrival. But this time, I realised you were not coming. I sat on the bed listlessly, fighting with my disappointment, not so much at the fact that you were not there but at the realisation that the other coast across that expanding moat, the coast of our living room, was further than I thought. I was already a bit out of breath, and the thought of swimming back straight away was too much. I was disappointed with myself—perhaps with my lack of fitness or purpose, I don't know exactly—and I dithered on the island, softening the creases of the bedspread and looking around thinking of decor improvements.

And then I saw you standing at the other end of the bridge, the living room end. The distance was too large to tell for sure, but I think your arms were on your waist, a smile on your face half-mocking, half-endearing, and then you shouted across, what are you doing there? I tried to reply but there seemed to be a delay across the sound, and then I heard you again, come back, dinner's ready, you said, and then moved back into the living room, shaded by the coming evening.

## waterspeak

I am distance.

These two have already discovered this. I am not
sure they like it.

But I like it.

I am distance. I like saying it. It sobers me up when
I get too embroiled in their daily shenanigans.

I am distance. It rolls off the tongue, like a tennis
ball sliding off an arm and reaching across the court.
I need to say it often, otherwise I risk becoming a little schizoid. You know how your schizophrenics paint
me, sweeping and vast, great oceans and open seas,
a breathing space from impulses, walls of openness
against the flood of the ego—well, that.

I am distance.

But I am also closeness. Connection, propinquity,
flatness, and flow. Continuum.

I am all this *and* I am also distance. I am both vast
and vertiginous, and asphyxiating, and intrusive. I
measure space in my own manner, faster and deeper than light, still excited about the way I spread my
elastic body and ravish up all little planetary bumps
and gravity-thick holes. My miles and years are
immense but syncopated, skipping from one evapo-
ration to the next, plunging from one gathering to
the next, until we,
all my we,
all my othernesses,
all my distances and propinquities,
all of all there is,
we get together, in one eternal interstellar crowd of
aeons without history.

I sandwiched these two humans between my great binary.

I mean, they asked to be there, thinking that it might be a snug, a little boudoir of exotic lovemaking.

But that's not how it works.

They are so pathetic, sweating to keep my sides apart, desperately spreading their puny arms and trying to hold off the tides of my paradox from folding into each other.

They are doing what all humans do:
they compartmentalise me.

Only they do not use bottles and dams. They go deeper—annoying little gnats—and try to split my molecular pride, my fierce identity of madness: they try to keep my distance apart from my closeness.

In vain.

Far from me from being vindictive. But here is a little demonstration.

**Part II**

*Where We Collapse Into Each Other*

## collapse: the lovers

We finally decided to hang that painting. It had been lying on the floor, leaning against the wall until we found time to deal with it. It was not a simple affair. The sense of distance, centre, and balance varied wildly between us, and every time we tried to hang something on the wall, we ended up spending a disproportionate amount of time swapping places between holding the thing and walking backwards to see the thing, arguing about what we both considered measurable, beyond-doubt facts that were nonetheless being communicated inaccurately, "just a little further up and to the right—no, just a little I said! It's too high now".

During one of those long moments, when I was holding the painting and you were looking at it from the sofa, my arms already aching and my legs restlessly twitching, I saw your face changing to an expression of somnolent awe, your eyes fixed on the painting but hazy, as if you were recalling last night's dream. I was ready to shout, what now? thinking that I had let it slip again and that we had lost what you considered its perfect place, when I felt my fingers being patted by a light mist, sticky yet cool to the touch. Even the odour of the room had changed, almost violently, into a marine potpourri of wetness. I turned towards the wall and nearly fell over, through it, outwards, narrowly avoiding an accident by clinging onto the painting to regain my balance. I do not know what would have happened had I fallen. You rushed over, pulling me in with too much force, landing on the floor, you first, me on top of you, painting cast somewhere to our side. We sat there, huddled, unable to think, marvelling at the spectacle, invaded by a sense of dread that was not altogether fatal, not altogether horrid.

*I am inside.*

The wall had blossomed into a leaking gash. Translucent swathes of thick liquidity were hanging from floor to ceiling, spreading where the wall was. The whole thing was gently trembling but without collapsing: a light frothy mist the only thing secreted from it. There was no cascading waterfall or sheets of rain invading our living room, no leak escaping or puddle gathered. It was as if the surface of a lake had suddenly turned vertical without spilling a drop, a gravity-defying elevation that retained its flatness. It could be mistaken for a projection, like those fake-nature screensavers complete with forest sounds. Except that our projection was not that sophisticated: there was no sound of water, lapping lake waves, or splashes from diving birds. Rather, it brought all the outside sounds in, magnified them as if they had passed through a boombox, tangled them like mixed up sheets of music, sharpened them as if sculpting them out of odoriferous metal, and thrusted them in our living room at a distorting volume. We could no longer recognise this megaphonised outside, a brash symphony of noise that had been eclipsed ever since the waters.

*I am continuum.*

That wall, translucent and magnifying, could no longer separate us from the outside. It could no longer fulfil that function. It stood there as a liquid memento of dry times, nursing a nostalgia for when we used to open the windows and had to tolerate the traffic noises from the street below. It brought all this back in an ironic way, as if its passage through the thickness of the water wall revealed its unbearable irrelevance.

*I am multiple.*

But there was another function to the wall which we only understood when we touched it. We did not even have to slide our hands through it—lightly touching it with the end of our fingers was enough: we realised we were utterly exposed. A two-way waterfall, the wall was opening us up to the outside, mixing our flat and ourselves with the falling evening. Where did our flat end? Where did our skin extend to? The wall was no longer separating but was rather bringing us together with the city. It had turned into a conduit between inside and outside, a passage rather than a block, pores rather than skin. Its outside and its inside had merged into one uniform, jellied conductor, bringing together two waters that we had always, up until then, thought different: our water, the water of our love and our domesticity, the water of our days and nights together, all that liquidity that we had welcomed in our relationship ever since we met that day with that small accidental puddle of sparkling water between us, all the waters in our bodies and the way we strove for them to flow together, to listen to each other and swirl in unison; and, on the other hand, this other water, the water of the flooded city, a city that had to reinvent itself constantly, allowing its guest to change it from its very foundations, to make it cling on to its verticality while casting wistful glances at the endless liquid horizon. These two waters, the two sides of our wall, had nothing separating them.

*I am one.*

Upon touching it, and later on, little by little, especially in the evenings when the surface was becoming calmer, the noise was dying down, the smells were abating and the light from the outside was turning softer and infinitely more tender, we were ushered into a state of alert confusion, where this and that side of the water flowed into each other and layerlessly mixed.

We were asleep when we felt the shake. At the time we did not know that this was in some way the end, or perhaps a new end, even more cataclysmic than the end that the waters had brought. We jumped out of bed and ran to the windows to see what had happened. The waters were agitated, waves crashing on the facades, spray spluttering all the way up to the higher floors. People on windows and balconies, some shouting. Did you feel it? Was that really an earthquake? And then, some deeper, unuttered cries: was this the return of the earth, the earth claiming the surface and overthrowing that wet blanket that had been covering it all this time? And where would the water go?

*I am already.*

We imagined a cosmic tsunami, volumes of water being catapulted out of the planet and into deep space, liquid continents standing erect for a long interstellar moment and then evaporating, swallowing up the moon and extinguishing the sun. Oh yes, we were imaginative in our panic. In those days, we were progressively getting used to almost automatically linking our own experiences with the life of the planet at large—not so much in that usual, anthropocentric way of believing that what we did was decisive for the planet, nor in the romantic, human-absorbed way of asking whether reality exists if we shut our eyes. No, we were past both these states, increasingly convinced of our definitive departure from the centre of the planet, wherever that was. We were just becoming aware of our new place, a thread amongst the multiplicity of threads that made up the planetary knitwork. And so our imagination would fly far and high every time something unusual occurred.

The shaking had stopped, but a vibration could still be felt as if a giant hand was tapping the surface of the water somewhere far away, a music of skins pulsating through our planetary tympanum and reaching us echo-like. And then there were these clouds of fine dust that we noticed for the first time in a very long time, a memento of the days of cars and street dirt, of dusters and hoovers. The source of the dust was to the right of our building, and so too was the rumbling sound, now joined by more agitated voices. And then, just like that, things calmed down, the dust settled and drowned, the noise slept off, the water softened out. We craned our necks but could not see anything. We could only read the faces of our neighbours in front of us, themselves probably reading other faces further down the line.

Whatever it was, it was a disaster of the kind we were no longer used to. After the waters, big events, whether positive or negative, seemed to have stalled, their magnitude reduced to a locality to which only those nearby had access. We had no means of knowing what was happening outside our city or even outside our immediate neighbourhood. The little we found out, we did through others.

*I am closeness.*

And so with this. Deep amidst the panic-stricken reading of faces, signs, sounds, and movements, someone must have shouted clearly enough for the neighbours opposite us to hear and repeat: the large white tower at the end of the avenue had collapsed. The tower was a vast complex of a structure, with inner courtyards and atriums and several interconnected buildings dedicated to mixed commercial and residential use. After the waters and the shutting down of companies, most floors were converted to apartments occupied by residents of other buildings who had been attracted by the solid security that the tower seemed to promise. Although its famous ludic facilities were obviously reduced to empty spaces, it remained a coveted building and was quite densely occupied even by the standards of this new reality of reduced residents. The catastrophe then must have been truly gigantic.

We dressed up hastily and went down to the third floor. It took us a while because of the darkness and the people who had had the same idea as us. Or perhaps it was not an idea but an urge, a thrusting out, a fear of belonging to a future that was as inhospitable as that bellowing night—whatever it was, we were all there, fumbling along the rickety gangways till we reached a point closer to the area that used to be covered by the white tower buildings. Most of the buildings had collapsed—whether all together or in a sequence setting off a causal chain of collapse was not clear. A sprawling rubble range was peeking out of the waters like a rugged island in the middle of a sleepy ocean. Some people had already been hard at work, holding large torches that criss-crossed the rubble like some sort of laser sky celebration, trying to find survivors.

*I am depth.*

We were helplessly looking on, standing on our planks, unable to cross over since all the boats in our building had crossed over with the first wave of volunteers. In the beams of light falling on the rubble were illuminated the ghosts of our illusions: chunks of walls, kitchen sinks and torn-out sofas, clothes, and even food, all piled on top of each other and all of them topped by protruding pieces of metal sticking up like flagless poles. All this was signalling the one thing shared by everyone who was standing there witnessing the aftermath: alongside the hundreds of people buried under the rubble, slowly eaten by the waters and the sheer weight of the verticality that used to stand there, our very own bodies were also lying, barely breathing, waiting for a salvation that was never going to arrive.

## collapse: waterspeak

We are one. Inside and outside, death and depth, them and me.

This is the end of the illusion.

That little, polite, domesticated water, all rippled purring and soft streams, shut behind their flat doors and sculpted into memories of summers, is no more.

This is the end of choice.

Sweet lovebirds, bane of my grandiosity, crown to my wafting mane!

Get ready to flatten your plump bodies, open your comfortable mouths, and swallow up my every drop: salt and weed, piss and snot.

What you have always feared to be true, you finally know.

No use locking the door at night: I am already inside. No point in carrying me around in plastic baubles like some sort of talisman: I am already polluted. Sorry, but the excreta have hit the fan.

We are all drenched.

I am doubling up, my swell rounds and bloats, I become my own flotsam, I stretch my body to the end of the unthought and fold myself back to their everyday, a mobius strip of saturation.

I am in me and there is nothing but it.
We are all drenched.

You are screaming in hydropathic paroxysm, soaking in irreversible saturation. No one is privileged anymore, no prior invitation can save you. Our bodies are intertwined for good, and you will henceforth strive to balance on my surfaces, cityless, humanless, prideless, gill-less, breathless.

And please no more dramas of the Edenic type. It's been ages since the last apple was sold in the night markets of your drowned cities. And you'd better start avoiding walls—you know, collapse and all... So please don't start imagining bad daddies expelling you from the kindergarten. It's all you, shoving and pushing, cramming the gates as if you hadn't caused enough trouble already. Forget any apocryphal stories about your Adam signing contracts with snakes in the middle of rivers, stranded in undulating despair and wishing he had never left.

It is done, and there shall be no seconds.

# Part III

*Where We Merge*

## one

The thud of the tower jolted us out of a period of calm which we only appreciated in retrospect. Before the collapse—during that indefinable stretch of time that came once the initial surprise, fear, and even panic of the waters had settled—a calm surfaced like steam rising from below. We were enveloped against all odds in a softly-earned, fragile serenity. Yet we could never fully indulge it. Perhaps because we were aware of the fact that this was not normal, that we should have been feeling differently: angst-ridden and rebellious rather than appeased by this feeling of estranged calmness. The calm was opening up almost away from us, at arm's length, a spectacle we were observing as if someone else was meditating in front of us and we were feeling at peace vicariously. We might have been present in a process of planetary mindfulness, watching from the sides and allowing the waves of that submerged sphere of ours to lap against our skins—but we were not there yet.

Then came the collapse. Whatever calm we had felt, it was now receding. The fall of the tower had the effect of a shaft thrust deep into the body of the city, changing it, and us, forever. Life in the city, our building, and our flat had become anguishing; we were constantly in waiting, loomed over by the next catastrophe. It is difficult to believe now that, at the time, we had no inkling of the fact that foundations across the globe were being eroded, that those unshakable pillars propping up our hubris were turning out not to be waterproof. Yet we had not thought of it, or at least no one talked about it. Was that another manifestation of our delusion of omnipotence? Of our supposed capacity to adapt to whatever was thrust at us, to negotiate life and death and all their difficulties in a not too onerous manner? Was this the final test for our presumed ability, as a species but also as individuals, to charm whatever we could not forcefully conquer? We had managed so far to negotiate our way with the waters, with the collapsed structures, with the increasing lack of services, even with the uncertainty of when and whether the waters would rise further. But this was a blow that we could not negotiate: it was not just a building collapsing, however illustrious a symbol of the city the tower might have been. Rather, it was our own verticality collapsing, our final raft against the horizontality of the undifferentiated.

This was our absolute fear: of becoming one with everything. And here is the strange thing: previously we had flirted with this idea of oneness, taking pleasure in imagining ourselves to be part of the waters, even lamenting the fact that we could not become more liquid ourselves. All that was only a beautiful idea kept at bay precisely because of its impossibility. But now the horizontal has become a very real possibility, shedding all its previous signifieds of beauty, higher belonging, or aquatic utopia, and becoming instead only one thing: death. And while the death augured by the collapse of the tower was a collective death, an expiration of human life as we knew it—indeed the beginning of the end for our beloved verticality—what made it even more concrete and therefore unbearable was the fact that death would be parcelled out individually, for each one of us who was still opting to remain. This death would be felt by every single one of us one day—or even worse one night—like a scream that would start high up, suspended above the earth at an artificial distance, and would then precipitate downwards, pulled by dusty rubble and the dismembered remains of civilisation, only to be drowned in the lurking waters below. We realised that our building might be next, waiting in the queue to pay its respects to the city's most eminent guest—not water anymore, but extinction.

two

As early as the day after the collapse, we started noticing the cracks. They seemed to appear all over the walls in the flats and the corridors. We started obsessing about them, even pre-existing ones. Previously invisible paint cracks, or marks from long-forgotten antediluvian attempts at hanging pictures on the wall, were now immediately harking to structural problems—indisputable indications of foundational imbalances, sources of obsessive focus and infinite anguish.

One morning we woke up to a dripping sound. Water was trickling from a small but now bloated crack on the living room ceiling. It could have been concentrated humidity reaching boiling point and distilling into a small indoor cascade. It could have been a fixable leak. It could have been another manifestation of the outside forcing itself in. But it could also have been something much more sinister: it could be the beginning of our building's collapse.

I rushed breathlessly upstairs and knocked on the neighbours' door. Toby, a young man whom we had seen before but never spoken to, answered the door. After listening to my rather agitated questions, he let me in, politely but diffidently. He had an air of being interrupted for a trifle. I noticed he was handsome in a faraway mode, as if unable to communicate his beauty directly. While explaining the reason for my agitation, I realised that Cinder was also there. I was a little surprised, but I could not tell why. I did not know that they were friends, although there was no reason why they wouldn't be. Cinder was standing with his hands in his pockets, observing us unperturbed and somewhat enjoying our exchange. With a slightly irritating smirk, he explained that a leak would be out of the question: it'd been a long time since those tubes had had any water in them. I know, I said, but what if the water had somehow found a way in and started eating the building from within? Is that so difficult to imagine? They reluctantly helped me look around and try to locate the underfloor tubes by knocking around on the parquet, but there was indeed nothing in Toby's flat that could have caused the leak—there was only a sofa right where the water would be leaking from, no bathroom or kitchen or anything of that sort.

They both offered to help with the leak, or whatever it was. We came back downstairs and found you placing all the buckets we had in the flat to catch the pouring water. We stood around, the four of us looking rather helplessly at the ceiling, green aquarelle spreading in concentric circles, and from the middle a softly singing summer rain leaking out, dense and cascading but with a lack of deliberateness, a sort of resignation—as if the initial direction had been different, horizontal or slanted perhaps, but in the process had somehow given up and allowed itself to be carried downwards by gravity.

The buckets were filling up quickly, and Toby was helping to carry and empty them. He was obviously doing it under protest, however: all the while he talked about his fear of contagion from the waters, the mosquitoes that were apparently mutated and lethal, the plants that some people were eating but were venomous because of the underwater dirt, the rust coming out of the reservoir's tap—the list went on. These were all issues we had thought about before but to which we had somehow not paid much attention. With Toby's incantations, though, they felt grave and urgent. All of a sudden, the world turned into an even more inimical place. If we were not killed by the collapse of our building, we would die of some sort of terrifying disease. A form of dusty panic started settling upon us, as if our skins were crawling back, tightening us in rather than opening us up to this porous communication we had felt recently. I tried to catch your eye when we passed each other in the corridor with buckets, partly to reassure myself—but it was too brief, we were too distracted, it felt faraway.

Toby suggested we cracked the ceiling open to find where the leak was coming from. I thought it was a mad idea and turned to Cinder for support, but he was nowhere to be seen—he must have walked out earlier. You, however, seemed willing to try. You brought the ladder from the balcony and climbed up, hammer in hand, head almost touching the ceiling.

But you stopped short of knocking. You stood there, eyes up, as if drawn in by the green circles, water streaming on your face, and us two holding the ladder in place and waiting for you to start.

You did not.

You stepped back down, placed the hammer on the floor, raised your hand and touched my cheek, water on water, the pores of our skin still open, skin that bridged rather than separating us, skin melting into each other's openness. Toby asked us whether we were all right, and I answered, yeah sure, let's wait before we start wrecking it all, it might stop soon anyway.

That evening, we stood in our living room rain, bathing under a gentle gravity that was taking us deep into our floor and all the way to the floors below us. We felt spread out and connected, momentarily forgetting our fears.

The following morning, the leak had dried completely. The building would survive another day.

### three

In the week after the collapse, a veritable exodus took place. People started moving out of the city en masse. Some people from our building decided to move to neighbouring ones that looked more solid, although we had no means of knowing what the criteria of solidity might have been. After all this time in the water, all buildings looked tired, dipped in mossy abandon, sticky with a promise of dereliction. Everyone was suffering from some sort of edificial hypochondria, exchanging panic-inducing comments about cracks, creaking sounds, imperceptible but surely meaningful floor movements. This was slowly becoming indistinguishable from the other, already diffused, form of hypochondria. One afternoon, I decided to visit Lorna and Marek's increasingly empty and quiet shop on the third floor. I usually checked in with them once a day, but that day I was feeling especially lonely, perhaps in need of a consolation that could not be found either in our usual withdrawal or in the little routines we had established in the house. Lorna was standing behind the counter, seemingly waiting for something or someone. She was wearing that dissociated look she often had during the last few weeks, and I knew better than to try and engage her in conversation. I could not see Marek in the shop. I liked Marek very much—he was always easy to talk to. His deep sense of responsibility, proven several times over the past few months, never seriously interfered with his seemingly inexhaustible capacity for small talk. Part of me wanted to meet him, ease my loneliness, perhaps talk about a red seaweed recipe he had given us and which we had tried with little success. I walked further in the shop, hoping to bump into him working under some heavy foliage. I stooped beyond the wild viscous canopy of the entrance and slowly made my way towards the second room, which by now was so dense with vegetation that one had to climb over branches and piles of roots in order to make even a little headway. That room always offered a deeper sense of safety and calm, despite its thick humidity and muddy surfaces.

Marek was nowhere to be seen. But just inside the room, crouched beneath a particularly large branch jutting out of the central willow tree, Toby seemed to be hiding. As soon as he saw me coming in, he turned to me like a scared animal. I gave him a non-committal smile, heartfelt but also a bit formal, appeasing: no need to be scared, offer for companionship extended but without fetters, do what you will with it, I am fine either way. He responded with a small oblique grin, to me but also to no one in particular, touching his cheek with his right hand, retreating ever so slightly deeper into the foliage. I thought I had read this right and softly moved on when I noticed that he had brightened up, as if he had suddenly remembered something. I turned and saw him motioning me into his alcove. Half- convinced by his bright gesture, half-coerced out of a sense of kindness, I walked in and sat next to him, making myself as comfortable as possible on a pile of dried leaves. Toby was likeable, albeit also elusive and often agitated. We had grown fond of him in the few days immediately after the leak, but we still knew very little about him. At that moment I was hoping for some gentle camaraderie on an easy, even superficial, level: nothing too heavy, no future talk, no fear of collapse, just a soft, quiet togetherness. It was the garden shop after all, a place of recollection and calm resolve.

But Toby was clearly agitated, unable to let go even in that green womb. He started talking once again about illnesses and what he saw as his fragile health in that urgent manner that he had when he was going on about these issues. He asked me whether I knew of a doctor. I mentioned Selina. She had recently emerged as our de facto building doctor, recalling whatever she could from her mother's old medical practice and combining it with her interest in the medicinal qualities of the unsurprisingly abundant seaweed. Toby nodded, yes I know, but he was clearly not satisfied. He carried on talking in a tense but still distant manner: I am just worried, nothing specific, but with all these viruses doing the rounds, we are powerless against these new bacteria, and what happens if one gets ill, where can one go? He seemed immured in a hypochondriac swirl, the kind we have been encountering more and more often in the people around us. Many seemed to be poised between the fear of a symptom being something much more serious than just a passing ailment, and the need to focus on something other than the waters.

This was a different form of resistance to our surrounding reality. It was a self-perpetuating and insular reaction, leading to an infinitely more distressing isolation than the usual folding-in we were all experiencing. Toby was clinging onto an undoubtable need to carry on being alive. But he was

also clinging onto a different, perhaps opposed, desire. He wanted to carry on in the way our bodies
used to be in the past, the way they used to be separated by skin and material instances of individual identity—little autonomous units of walking and
talking presence. His hypochondria was feeding his
desire for an antediluvian individuality. He still retained that illusion; he believed in it and would not
let go. He was in love with his symptom. And why
not? It protected him from this alarming sliding we
were all experiencing, this plunging deeper into the
great aquatic body, this becoming a drop amongst
drops in the open sea of the earth's waters.

To be in the middle of it all was not easy. We all felt
frightened, exposed, irreversibly sinking. Toby was
holding onto an illusion of choice: to remain dry or to
succumb to the wetness. But it did not help him—he
was becoming even more vulnerable, his supposed
choices even more self-sabotaging. He was regularly driven into whirls of panic, full-blown crises
that were conjuring a future too much to behold,
where his body and the building were merging into
one vast fragility. We would hear him pace up and
down or even run across his flat overhead, banging
on walls like a bat caged in a metal box, all aflutter
and screeching. Cinder seemed to be with him during some of these crises and loud arguments could
be heard, usually ending with Cinder's storming out
and banging the door. It was not easy to calm Toby
down. Whenever we tried, and we did try a couple of
times, we were also plunged into this contagious panic, knowing full well that we could never tell when the
next mysterious fatal disease would devour us, discovering with frustration the baselessness of all our
assuaging arguments.

The only thing to repeat was, why not move out,
why not live somewhere else. But in all conversations
of that sort, even with others less taken by fear than
Toby, the question was met with various ways of de-
murring, with mental shoulder shrugging and eyes

cast to the side as if in search of the real reasons why we had all chosen—although it was not a choice and had never been presented as a choice either to ourselves or to others—to remain. The only one who was openly and almost laughingly dismissing any suggestion of moving was Lorna. She would always say, in a rather too-defiant and somewhat out of place way, that she would go down when the building went down. She was probably the only one amongst us who had come to terms with the possibility of a watery life that was soon to be interrupted by a watery death. She seemed to have settled in her own hierarchy of priorities, where the plants in her shop and her daily diving were of much greater importance than the continuation of her previous way of life. But the rest of us were still struggling, torn between, on the one hand, an etiolated desire to stay put—covered as we were by this blanket of permanent humidity that could only be resolved with a violent collapse—and, on the other, a rather blind but at least proactive dash to escape, to run away, to allow ourselves the luxury of another world.

We found ourselves falling deeper in an infernal cycle of repetition. Our initial choice to remain in the city when the waters first rose was followed by a stubborn, fractal repetition of that same choice even when mounting challenges were making our everyday unbearable. Whatever the circumstances, it seemed as if the first proclamation to stay put was being reiterated every time. We were of course aware of the nonsense of all this: there has never been a real choice. There had never been a moment when we actually had choices, alternatives, options. Our 'decisions' were simply absences of movement, a static momentum that led to nothing but an acquiescence masquerading as choice. We never even vocalised it as a choice. Our minds were never involved in this process. We only embodied it, our bodies carrying it around as if it were a gift whose origin no one could remember. Our own bodies were seemingly deciding to stay, but then again, not really—no decision there either, just not moving, not going away, not trying to save themselves despite our chattering minds urging our bodies to do precisely that. And this lack of movement, this most dramatic of refusals, the same as all the others before it but infinitely deeper, was the final push down a spiral of repetition.

Even practically, this move was difficult to imagine. Where would one go? Some had suggested that we start erecting tall stilts and building refuges on them. Even if a collapse were to take place, nobody would be hurt as much as when trapped in a crumpling building. But this required a technology that no one around seemed to have developed, or to have heard of anyone that had. The stilts would have to be exceptionally long and sturdy, and even if we could use some of the submerged tree trunks or electricity poles that used to line our avenues, we would never be able to place them sufficiently deep in the waterbed that they would withstand all the subsequent building work taking place on them, in addition to the pressures of water currents and the usual water erosion.

Another oft-discussed solution was to move to boats, be that to large rafts covered with makeshift roofs or to actual boats converted into homes. Even these, however, would not be fully secure. How far from a building ought one to moor so as to be protected from any collapse? And how exposed would that make one to the elements, to random violence, to passing criminals, or simply to people who might want to upgrade their own boat? The boat discussions had resurfaced in earnest, especially now that a boat had moored permanently just outside our building. Whenever we looked out of the windows, we were filled with a strong desire mixed with a deep melancholy. The boat was owned by an old woman, rugged, solitary, and aloof, who hardly exchanged a word with any of us beyond what was absolutely necessary. She seemed to be self-contained, more than any of us was at the time. Her command of her boat, her strict daily routine, her almost boastful ephemerality, even the way she interacted occasionally with the passing boats, was like a choreography of contentment and self-reliance. The desire to be in her place was strong; it would gallop in us like a storm, intense and abrupt and unavoidable, especially at night when things were creaking around us and the future appeared even shorter than we imagined during the day. We would all then look outside our windows and fantasise about being free and mobile, ready to sail off at the first sign of difficulty—even though several of us were ready to point out that if *we* were to go down, this woman would go too under all the debris collapsing onto her.

But even in its most luminously pure form, the desire was always trumped by the melancholy that giving in to flatness would entail. We were attached to a still strong sense of wanting to float above it all. We couldn't deal with the sadness of giving up the possibility of a theological vantage point from which to observe. We wanted to stay high up, propped up in our flats, close to the sky, attached to our human exceptionalism.

Small, powerless gods, all of us, drowning in our delusion of omnipotence.

For we still believed then that if there was something worse than losing to death, it would be losing our perspective on death.

**four**

The stress is proving too much for everyone. Everyone, in their own way, is deteriorating. You've always had some latent breathing problems, a mild case of asthma often exacerbated by panic attacks. But recently it has been getting worse. And tonight, a week after the collapse, it has reached the worst point I have seen. No amount of pills, hot drinks, or propping up of pillows has made it better. Some nights are always longer than others, I have come to accept that; I have been there, sitting up next to you in bed, watching you with various degrees of pity, resentment, worry, and affection, trying to forget myself and turn to you only, to reverberate with your breathing, your timing in life. But that night, each minute had a dream-like duration, with long lives lived between each impossible rattle and horizons of solitude folded into each attempt either of us made to go back to sleep.

We gave up and knocked on neighbouring doors in the hope that someone would help us get to the hospital. Marek, who lived in the flat right above the shop, opened immediately, wide awake as if waiting for our knock, almost reproachful for the notional delay. He helped us down, coolly balancing my distress and your pallor, hardly saying a word but with a gestural reassurance and efficiency that calmed me. We stepped out onto the planks through the heavy iron hatch doors that shut us all in during the night. Marek has effectively become the guardian of the building, opening and shutting these gates, keeping them secured with a few large iron bars. He seemed to be the only person who could manage these doors alone, and so he became the go-to resident when one wanted to go out or come in when the doors were shut.

Marek pushed the launch out while jumping in. The launch rocked wildly, suspended mid-city on the dark water, with us holding onto its edges as if still deep in a nightmare. He started rowing at a steady rhythm, impossibly slow I thought: more like someone practising a hypnotist's trick than someone who needs desperately to reach what passed for a hospital at those times. Faster, I thought, push it, I thought, give it to me, I thought but did not say, still trying to suppress my panic, shivering while wrapped in my crumbling sense of gratitude.

But you had calmed down, your breathing following the steadiness of Marek's rowing, synchronised with the sliding of water on the wooden surfaces. You sounded much better now, and for a moment I let go and listened to the city's veins pulsing along the same rhythm as your breathing and our rowing. There were long intervals of apnoea where the waters stood on hold, bloated with anticipation in glistening dark slopes, only to deflate and cascade with a hiss at the next breathing gasp, cautiously placing our skiff at the bottom of the swell. Marek's rowing was helping you more than I could. A small rocking sense of inadequacy washed over me.

With some effort, I turned to your breathing again, focusing on every permutation of its ebbing and flowing. Your head kept on falling on your shoulder, heavy with exhaustion, unable to counter the movement. I tried to hold it up and place it against the boat's interior. I even got up to put a folded scarf under your head, balancing without thinking on the rocking boat, emboldened by my role, used by now to the water, or so I thought. At that point, the boat swerved violently to avoid a protruding pole or something. I lost my balance, dizzied by the illusion of aquatic familiarity. Right then, like an automaton's last gesture before it winds down completely, your arm, surging from your comatose battle for air, darted up and got hold of me, stopped me from falling overboard, protected me. You steadied me. Even when you were not there, you still were there. Oblivious, one with the nocturnal city spread, deep in the fold of the water's breath, walled in a wheezing anxiety, yes, all that, but you were still there.

And then I realised: my role was not only to love you, to turn to you and care for you. My role was also to be loved by you.

We arrived in front of an awning lit by oil lamps. It probably used to be a window on the third floor of the hospital, but it was now a much amplified entrance. The awning was large enough for the launch to sail into what used to be the main hospital building and now seemed more like a network of badly-lit waterways formed between raised platforms piled up with rubbish. There was a long queue of vessels ahead of us. Progress was very slow. Some, clearly knowing their way round, were veering to the left or to the right, along even narrower waterways leading deeper into the belly of the sprawling building. We asked the woman steering the boat in front of us whether she knew where we could go for some urgent attention, but she did not know. We waited, stuck in that pulsating restlessness until the way was somehow liberated, and we moved into a sort of indoors port filled with vessels docked along its wharves. The air was caving in under the odorous clouds of disinfectant, anguishing wafts of fresh blood, restless bouquets of desolation. Going deeper in, we saw about eight or ten of what looked like medical stations, with some beds and equipment lying about. Most of them were abandoned except for two stations around which there seemed to be large throngs of people waiting to be seen. We docked and made our way to the closest station, with Marek shouting that we needed to be seen urgently. The crowd did not seem to move, however. Their backs were forming a wall around what was presumably the doctors' area. No one turned, no one even seemed to register the new arrivals, and we were left hovering around the thronging circle of people trying to find an opening to squeeze in.

I was holding you by one arm and Marek by the other, a cumbersome trio that could not fit in anywhere with ease. I motioned you to stop and rest against the wall. We placed you upright against a wall shiny with moss and humidity. I sat next to you, holding your hand and breathing with you, while Marek tried to push in to get hold of a doctor. He emerged a few minutes later with a big smile on his face and two large oxygen bottles under his arms. I was so happy I let go of your hand and started clapping, almost jumping up and down. It felt like a triumph after all that desperate pushing and waiting. Marek winked, justly pleased with himself, and helped me connect you to the breathing tube.

You calmed down immediately, as if the mere knowledge of having just a bit more oxygen was enough.

You breathed through the tube for a while, getting stronger by the minute. We decided to make our way back, since there was clearly nothing left to do there. We picked up the bottles and slowly walked back to the launch. You smiled and said, I think this needs to change. I can no longer rely on oxygen bottles.

I have to find another way of breathing.

My initial reaction to this was to look at you as if you were losing your mind. I had no idea what you meant and became even more worried. But your stare was serious. You actually meant it, to find another way of breathing. For some time now, our bodies had been feeling different, at the same time resisting and adapting to the new environment. Breath remained breath, but all of a sudden, amidst that panicked mob in the wet darkness, my body felt ready to accept the idea that there might be other ways of breathing. Whereas our sense of smell had become keener, some of our other senses had become less vital: our vision, for example, was becoming blurrier, and we would often need to rub our eyes to clear the film of water that seemed to have set up home there. On the other hand, our sense of touch was becoming much more sensitive and diffused, no longer limited to our fingers but tingling along our whole bodies, and it even felt—strange I know, I am not sure how to describe it—as if we were touching the inside of our bodies too, as if we were in closer contact with our organs and flows. At the same time, it seemed that we were breathing deeper and, how can I put it, inhaling more air these days. Not in some sort of breathing meditation way—there was nothing calm about it. It was more as if our lungs could feel that the air was about to be replaced by water and they were embarking on a futile resistance, storing up oxygen with longer and yet inevitably faster and more syncopated breaths.

So, when you said that you needed to find another way of breathing, I knew immediately that you were right. Not just for you: all of us had to find another way of breathing. I noticed my breath and how it had become an anguishing mirror of the collapse around us. We were resisting the inevitability of this new aquatic reality by hanging on to the *other* element: we resisted water by gulping up air. Marek started monkeying up the whole quick-breathing thing, making choking noises while waving his arms—a joke too far if it weren't for your new, open mood that allowed the light side of it to come through and for all three of us to start laughing like crazy. We were laughing quite simply because we realised the absurdity of this battle for air and how pointless it was to carry on in this way.

It wasn't as if it were all in the mind, though. There was no mental switch after which we would all be fine. Rather, as we were about to discover, it was a slow process that involved both conscious efforts and non-conscious actions. Above all, it involved others around us. It started with the three of us as we sailed back to our building. After our laugh, without addressing it explicitly but somehow in full awareness, we started breathing less, or perhaps not less but certainly no more than what we needed. We tried to eavesdrop on our respiratory needs, we tried to touch from within our air chambers and to breathe in only what was actually necessary. We resisted the need we had all had up until that moment to ingest more and more air, to succumb to that stressful hyperventilation that had become our way of being and had made everything worse.

We soon realised that the best way of doing this was to synchronise our breaths. We were overtaken by a much faster vessel and we were caught in the large volumes of water wake, so we all naturally held our breaths at the same time.

It was hard, and the temptation to go deep and panic again was strong, stronger in me than you, I noticed. But all that was needed was a lowering of the head, a nod downwards to where the dark glistening surface mirrored the luminous night sky, a breathing out ampler and deeper than any breathing in, and our breaths would converge again. From this airy merging, a fragile sail emerged that slid smoothly between the folds of the world as if there were no friction, as if we were finally part of this world and no longer its exception. We were trying to learn, slowly and even painfully, to share our breaths, collectively with each other and the world. But it would take a long time, with the threat of syncopation always around the corner.

## five

We kept on hearing stories about friends of friends who used to live in the white tower. We no longer had many contacts anymore, so it was either through neighbours or through Luz, who had become a frequent, almost daily visitor at ours. She would always bring news of the newly found dead and the survivors of the tragedy, hypotheses about why it happened, stories about what people had noticed in the days before the collapse and about how the tragedy was somehow predicted. And we would just sit there and listen.

In reality, though, this did not help us at all. We were already alarmed by anything sounding even vaguely like the haunting rumble that had swallowed up all these lives, and Luz's stories made us even more anxious. But she clearly needed to talk about it all, and we felt we had to listen. Her punishing revisiting of the events, with her face lighting up with an almost gleeful mania whenever any piece of news emerged, was probably her way out of depression and angst—futile, though, since she seemed even more agitated and depressed after having imparted the news. She sat there deflated and lost, a puddle of sadness by now a fixture around her armchair. She had changed dramatically after the collapse—just like most of us, of course. But her change seemed more serious because she was not bouncing back the way she used to do. This springing resilience was perhaps her main characteristic, her visiting card of sorts, announcing her arrival like a wave of contagious excitement even before she entered a room. But we noticed that even we were no longer taken by the irresistible anticipation that usually preceded her visits. Not because of their increased frequency but because of this general mood that left no one unscathed.

One evening, later than usual, Luz arrived with a man we had never seen before. He was slightly younger than her, warm and pleasant right from the start, taking in our inquiring stares in good spirit. Olalekan introduced himself with a confidence and directedness we realised we had missed. The waters had affected the way we interacted socially and especially those first instances of contact with someone we did not know. Without realising, we had all entered a mode of recoiling rather than reaching out, of speaking across a fog that separated our individual islands rather than walking up to the rare strangers that appeared in our lives. We felt we always needed some sort of reference, someone to have talked to us about them before, and well in advance too so that we would have time to process what we had heard and even to plan our behaviour. Olalekan landed into our lives that evening without any introduction.

This seemed especially odd once we realised that he and Luz were seeing each other. Luz's silence on the matter left us wondering how to react and whether to show our surprise or to pretend that we knew all along. She did not help us with this, leading us in neither direction and just letting us get on with each other. It turned out to be much easier than we initially feared, largely because of Olalekan's open manner. He spoke about the route they took to come here, complimenting Luz on her sailing abilities, seemingly unfazed by the darkness as if effortlessly attuned to all the vicissitudes of the waters around here. When we asked him where he lived, he turned to Luz and smilingly nodded towards her, mischievously implying that he was a burden she was kindly tolerating. She picked up on the joke and, after a few expected remarks about the use of the bathroom etc., she turned to us and said, Olalekan used to live in the tower.

This sentence, uttered so simply, sucked the breath out of the room. We managed to say nothing civil or sincere. We were fighting with a maddening sense of repulsion while feeling overwhelmed by the need to show compassion. He must have felt our unease, but he made no attempt to rescue us from the silence. We were trying to swallow the fear and nausea that his presence had started to bring down upon us, but it was as if we were trying to gulp back our own vomit. The waters had stripped us of the usual urge to conceal embarrassment—not in a conscious way but by obscuring that very embarrassment from us, making it hard for us even to notice it.

You reached for my hand across the sofa, a gesture visible to the guests, our sense of being threatened and our need to reach out for each other painfully obvious. There was no tender togetherness in this gesture, no 'be strong' message, no sadness before the facts.

It was simply and brutally a gesture of exclusion aimed at these two.

We wanted to reinstate our island, to erect a wall against this outside that was wedged into us so forcefully, even connivingly, as we felt then. Olalekan was not of course our first contact with death. But he was our first contact with survival from almost certain death. Instead of making us feel joyful with hope, it exposed us to the inevitability of death. And the fact that he was sitting in our living room, alive yet reeking of death, so close to our intimate little bubble of two, felt like a Trojan horse that managed to make its way in. We feared that we would lose our prized differentiation—already under attack from various sides—between us and them, between our love and the city outside. But above all we feared that we would lose this space between us—the only remaining promise of a future, the air that softly whizzes out when our bodies embrace, that sliver of private breath that remains when our skins glide flat against each other.

Luz was the first to speak, explaining in a slightly croaky voice how they met and, now almost justifying herself, how the best solution had been for Olalekan to move in with her.

The following day, Luz came on her own and sat down as if the previous night had never happened. We were too numb to ask, perhaps finally embarrassed by our dismay, and none of us referred to Olalekan. Only when we accompanied her to the door did we manage to mumble, say hi to Olalekan. A few days later, with a sense of relief tinged with fear that by now seemed inextricable from every interaction, we opened the door and welcomed both of them in. A new friendship started to blossom amongst us, tentative and much less laid-back than our initial jovial directness had set us up for. Yet, despite our softening, we were still not ready to welcome fully this reminder of death incarnate who, even in his story of survival (which we never learned), Olalekan carried around with him. We were not ready to forgive either ourselves for being so afraid or Olalekan, whose survival teased us with a burning hope we knew could no longer exist. At the time, we were consumed by the dreadful awareness that there was no future for us. It took us a long time to understand that the future we were living and fearing then was not the only possible one.

## six

It was one of those quiet afternoons when the water seemed unreal, a background decorative touch that will soon go away. You were at the window taking care of our potato and carrot plants, which had taken up most of our outside space. I was on the sofa facing you, reading a book from that pile of books we had in the flat which I had never so far bothered to read but which I had now finally got round to. I caught a movement and looked up. You were leaning out of the window, trying to make something out. Anything to distract me from the dull book, I thought, and joined you. You pointed at two pairs of legs swinging in the void out of a window quite a few floors below. We could only see the legs from the knees down, carefree stretching and swaying in the air as if they belonged to two kids trying out risky tricks while their mothers were not looking.

The strange thing was that those lower floors were, as far as we knew, uninhabited. Who are they? Do we know them? We must know them unless they are new-comers, but why would they go so low? The silent city carried our voices down. Two heads joined the legs and looked up towards us. With some difficulty we made out Cinder and Toby. We waved at them, slightly apologetically I thought, as if we were intruding. Toby hesitantly waved back, Cinder remained unrespon-sive. I raised my voice, this time speaking to them rather than about them: is everything all right? An inane question that I somehow felt forced to ask just to establish a connection. My voice echoed across as if in a theatre set, loud but unnatural. They nodded. Their heads disappeared back into the room, and af-ter a brief moment Cinder's head popped out again, smiling and motioning us to join them.

We looked at each other and shrugged: "why not?" We made our way down to the fourth floor. The main staircase of the building was fronted with windows that allowed some light to come in from outside. The fourth-floor corridor, however, was windowless. The whole floor was abandoned. The hallways were dark and damp, the floor covered in sludge and filled with rubbish and debris. Everything looked the same. Our nostrils were still full of stagnant water, our sense of smell dampened. It was very hard to make our way to where Cinder and Toby were. We tried several doors that we thought corresponded to the window we saw them in, but they were all locked or somehow blocked. One finally gave in, but the air was so full of cobwebs that it was impossible for someone to have walked through. We felt like giving up, but some-thing impelled us to carry on.

We weren't making it easy for ourselves. We never called them; we never made any more noise than absolutely necessary. They could have just called us in and guided us. But it was as if we purposefully avoided attracting their attention. We kept on trying various doors and walking into abandoned apartments as quietly as possible, at times even getting so disoriented that we could no longer tell which side of the corridor was the front one. It is not clear why we were behaving with such a misplaced discretion. We couldn't possibly have woken anyone up—it wasn't that late, and anyway the lower floors were empty. It had more to do with a sense of trespassing. Not into the apartments so much as on those two. There was something oddly intimate about the fact that they were both sitting there in the middle of the night on an abandoned floor looking out on a city submerged in water and darkness. It felt like they were reclaiming an aspect of the city to which we had no right. After a while, we even wondered whether we had actually imagined that hand waving us to join them.

Finally, a door opened just behind us. The corridor flooded with light. To our relief, Cinder, storm-lamp in hand, had just come to fetch us. He smiled and held the door for us, inviting us to remove our shoes. We complied unthinkingly, unquestioningly even, completely taken aback by what was spreading before us, a spectacle we could never have anticipated when we walked in. The apartment had been completely emptied of its previous content. The walls were all painted in a naive, almost childlike, way, with trees, little houses, gardens, and rivers in the foreground, and hills and blue mountains in the distance. They were interrupted by rolls of wallpaper placed here and there, seemingly randomly but with a certain regularity. These were reminiscent of rococo scenes, with exotic birds, chinoiserie, and little figures swinging from gem-studded branches, all floating on a golden red background. The theme carried on throughout the rooms, even the bathroom.

But the most extraordinary thing about it was that the whole apartment floor was covered in what by then had become the rarest of commodities: clean, soft sand. It was lying there barren, virginal, cleared of any weeds or plants, splayed up for our pleasure. We were invited to walk around barefoot, to sit or roll in it, to taste it and rub it against our skin, to pick it up in handfuls and throw it at each other. We were like kids seeing snow for the first time. Our joy was so infectious that Cinder and then Toby joined in, the four of us rolling in a red cloud that puffed and swirled all around us, inebriated with this almost primordial lack of wetness, unaccustomed to this carefully maintained dryness that allowed even dust motes to blossom into a perfectly round desiccation.

The frenzy ended up with all four of us having a breathless coughing fit, laughter and dust being a potent combination. We walked to the window and stood with our backs to the world, breathing heavily, our faces still beaming with ecstasy, marvelling at the way the dust veils were settling back to the floor. When we could start talking again, I asked . . . less than that actually, I just opened my arms, taking in the whole apartment, and looked at them with eyes wide open and mouth agape with a question, inviting them to say something but also allowing them to ignore my question, to take it as a sign of contented admiration and leave it at that.

But Toby, with a bright smile lifted straight from a playground, said, it was Cinder's gift to me, all of it, the whole thing, he was painting it for weeks, he found the wallpaper at that famous antique shop that was spread out on several floors at the other end of the city, and the paint tins somewhere who knows where, and the sand he brought bag after bag, multiple journeys over weeks from an old building materials yard that was lying submerged nearby, and he sprayed it, thinly at first so that it dried, and then topped it with still further layers until this feel of deep pure earth blossomed under our feet. While

Toby was speaking, Cinder took his hand and held it in his, occasionally bringing it up to his lips, embarrassed and proud in equal measure at this incandescent listing of his achievements. He finally spoke, making light of Toby's praises and adding that he had thought of it as a way to ease Toby's constant fear of infection. He wanted to create a utopia of crisp nostalgia, as disinfected and safe as possible, where the two of them could pretend that the world hadn't changed all that much after all.

Cinder had managed to keep the whole thing secret from Toby until he was able to present him with the finished product. Not only that, but they had also managed to hide it from everyone else all this time. We were the first ones to know, let alone to visit, they said. We never asked why this honour, why this special treatment. We had been invited right into their bubble of intimacy with each other and with a fantastical world. We could never have imagined it. From the outside, the whole thing seemed so unlikely because of how different the two of them were. But from within, to the extent at least that we could glimpse, it felt like a floating nest surrounded by the inescapable liquidity.

### seven

After that, we visited their dry playground a few times. It felt like our little illicit secret—probably because that's what it was. No one was to know, especially not Selina, Cinder's mother, or his father. This struck us as odd. We hadn't formed an opinion on his father, since he very rarely showed up and anyway hardly ever said anything, but Selina seemed at ease with Toby. Cinder had flourished in the past few weeks. He seemed much less morose and was consistently more talkative, not just with us but with the rest of the building too. Relationships of any sort, whether friendships, affairs, or family bonds, were becoming so rare that they were a cause for celebration.

At the same time, we could see why revealing their connection might be a problem. It had little to do with whom someone chooses as a best friend or lover, and more with the fact of the new connection. We were reminded of how awkward we felt when Luz introduced us to Olalekan. The presence of death was of course much heavier, the smell more pungent, in Olalekan—a survivor, perhaps the sole one or in any case one of very few, of the collapse of the tower. In Cinder and Toby's case, death was differently present. Intimate relationships were an obvious defence against the invading tides, a way of closing up and folding in. At the same time, however, they threw our exposure to the elemental and our utter unpreparedness before it into a much harsher light. Intimacy, and especially the kind that flourished after the waters, often felt forced and desperate. Even worse, it felt manifestly ineffective. However well one defended oneself against the suffering brought by the new reality, intimate connections, instead of alleviating this suffering, invariably aggravated it in the long run.

It was as if we were attacking the massive water wall of a tsunami with a beach toy, carving light incisions into the voracious tremor of its surface and hoping in vain to lessen its impact. Like most things that were trying to recreate a normality, this too often worked only as a reminder of how normality was forever lost.

Still, at other times the whole thing felt genuinely hopeful, a veneer-thin layer of optimism spread on the body of our collective melancholy.

But Cinder was adamant that his parents should not know, especially about their dry oasis. The truth was that it wasn't that difficult to keep it covered up. It was something so different to the wet normality of our days, so alien yet so deeply embedded in our bodies—a succulent, wet dream for the dry—that we could not even place it on the same level as or compare it with anything else. We all knew that this was a refuge and had to be kept that way, apart from the usual discussions about the waters, the uncertain future, and the collapsing buildings. So sometimes we would just play around, recovering a childhood of gardens and parks, which for most of us anyway was not even representative of our actual childhoods; or we would just sit and breathe in that way we had slowly become accustomed to, collectively and in unison, riding synchronous waves of air, feeling the world rocking along our breathing in the rhythm of our togetherness.

It was on one of those days: the windows wide open and the sun streaming in hot and soporific, the four of us spread like starfish on the floor, our eyes shut and our minds completing the fantasy with smells of cut grass and dung, sounds from a farm with cows mooing and wood being chopped, or even a city park with kids playing and pets running around. It was on one of those days that Cinder said, in a voice that seemed to come from within our fantasy—a faraway, slightly echoing voice that might once have carried a sense of urgency that had nonetheless faded by the time the voice finally reached us, like light from another star—in that voice Cinder said, we should leave. He did not mean to leave the flat. He did not even mean the building.

We all knew.

We had reached a limit on what we could still be and do under these conditions. Our brief dry spells, while full of delight, felt increasingly thin and fragile, incapable of extending their momentary therapeutic effect to the rest of our lives. We were gradually becoming aware that this dry escape was just a way back to the difficulty of a life we had not chosen. Instead of making easier and more tolerable what we had, this crisp earth under our bodies was becoming a crumbling reminder of what we could never have again. We would increasingly plunge deep into a messy, almost panic-induced seclusion after our dry games, each time finding it harder to float up and resume normal living. The joy of the dry flat had crash-landed us right there, before the limit.

To leave, then. But go where? In pursuit of what? Leave the city? Leave wetness in pursuit of real dryness? Somehow, nothing felt right. We were oscillating between contrasting desires that were masquerading as instincts. We were lost.

Yet Cinder's remark made sense to all of us. We sat up and started talking about it, each one suggesting different, equally untested ideas we had heard through the grapevine or through the people who used to return to the city after their explorations. But all these—the still-dry mountains in the north of the country, the tall colonies in the south that supposedly were open to new residents, or the floating arks that contained even animals and were like autonomous cities—all these had been obsessively talked about and equally definitively disproven so many times that after a while we all realised how tired the whole discussion was and we fell silent.

## eight

After that, time took on a fluorescent harshness. It was as if, all of a sudden, everything had been thrown into relief. We became aware of every passing moment—not in a grateful, being-in-the-present way but rather the opposite: we would spend our every present moment lamenting the misery of our past and fearing the threat of our future.

There was no present in our present.

Even when we were trying to escape the everyday by doing something out of the ordinary, we would mostly end up being reminded of the bleakness, which wrapped itself around us like a poisonous cloak.

We often relied on our memories of previous times. It was our way of communicating our tenderness towards each other. It was also a way of being tender towards ourselves, of allowing ourselves a breathing space from the relentless fight around us. We would reminisce, initially at length, but increasingly relying only on single words or on hints of scent to evoke the feeling of the remembered scenes. Yet, in spite of remaining the same, some memories seemed to be taking on a different hue, a different direction than the one we thought we remembered. It was as if happy memories from the past were being brought up in our angst-ridden present and were becoming tainted by it. It was as if the stories themselves were changing. Not our memory of them or our ability to recall them in a certain way, but the very stories were changing across time. It is hard to explain, but it seemed as if the present was colonising our past in such a way that the past simply could not survive the way it had done so far.

Take for example that late summer evening years ago. The last swim of the season, the sun still hot but gentle, softened up thanks to the turning of the globe towards autumn. We had decided to go to a different beach, one with a beach bar that was cool but down-tempo, west-facing with full view of the setting sun. We felt it would have been perfect for our last swim in the sea that summer, a celebration of sorts. And it was—it was all happiness and abandon, the beach bar buzzing in mellow Sunday vibes, people with drinks in hand stretched on white loungers facing the calm sea and waiting for the vast orange sky that would come in a matter of minutes. It was the per-fect early September Sunday, a little treat just before the usual return to work. It was also a farewell to a summer as slow and burning as any summer before that and, we thought, any summer after that. For the stretch of one evening, we felt we were admitted to the fold of infinity, to a line stretching out to a hori-zon able to accommodate all of us, for ever.

This is how we always remembered it, and we've often reminisced about that beach bar and that par-ticular evening. But recently our access to that mem-ory seems to have changed. The beach bar is still there, but everything else is different. Not that we remember it differently—we are sure that the way we remember it now is how it was, and we have relegated the previous memory to some sort of glitch: did we really remember it that way, how could we? Yes, a beautiful evening, but also a very difficult one, such melancholy. Our memory of the evening is saturated by a harsh yellow sadness. The beach bar is a little abandoned, a little past its best: the sun loungers are stained with the weight of a busy season, the white canvas tents are torn by unkind winds. The music is too harsh, too unresponsive to our anticipation of the sunset—but perhaps we are the only ones that really anticipate it. The rest of the crowd is probably doing something else, drinking and checking their mobile phones or whatever, but there is no frisson of antic-ipation, no consciousness of last swim, last evening, last sunset of the season—except perhaps for us.

We are lounging, though, drinks in hand, facing the sea, right next to where the waves break, away from the somewhat relentless beat of the DJ, on al-most the last cluster of sun loungers before the empty beach starts. Children are playing in front of us. One of them holds an empty green beer bottle, fills it with seawater, and, standing tall against the sun, his fig-ure extending in front of us and kindly shading us, he empties it back into the sea from a height, as high as his stretched arm will allow him, a gurgling laugh ac-companying his barman-type questions, Another one, madam? This is our best quality whisky, please try it! Have this one instead, it is even better! The game carries on for longer than any of us thought possible, a well of enthusiasm clearly feeding the boy's persis-tence, every waterfall a different one, every unan-swered question as exciting as the one that will follow.

He is about ten years old. He has his whole life ahead of him, a life so long and so infinite that it can accommodate this inane repetition of filling and emptying the bottle without the oppression of an ap-proaching end.

At that point—in reality or in memory I do not know—we realise that we will live less than him. That whatever age he is, he will, statistically speaking, most probably experience more of the future than we could ever experience. And just like that, the infinity of the evening turns, and with it the infinity of our lives—those long, uninterrupted lines carrying us into the future. That evening our life lines appeared before us and the comparison was dramatic. While his line stretched long and straight, ours was ending much earlier, our final point waving goodbye to his continuing stretch. Our line has never really been infinite. Just a short breath with a beginning and an end.

Previously, when the memory was still luminous and soothing, we remembered that we had stayed on until the sea became that deep, almost red-orange, our swimming bodies sliding in the calm of the evening, doused in a lush promise of everlasting warmth. But now we remember it very differently. We actually know what happened; this is the real memory, we think, no, we know. What happened was that we left well before the sunset, chilled to the bone by a westerly wind that agitated the sea and made us all irritable.

### nine

Cinder's urging to leave affected us deeply. It was an invitation to voyage we could no longer ignore. Our bodies were becoming increasingly restless, our spaces increasingly narrow. Perhaps our anxiety about the building collapsing had finally turned into a sort of flight impulse. We were aware that, if we were to dare this flight, a readiness was required, some geographical knowledge, some reacquaintance with our bodies in movement, a cartographic will in anticipation of the vastness that was summoning us.

Things started changing between us, too. We had hardly seen the rest of our neighbours in the previous few days, as if we had become reluctant to seek out company. Our days and nights together had become softer and more precious, round comfort bubbles of intimacy that kept us busy with each other. We spent long hours talking about things we had stopped talking about since the waters. We revisited books and images, we rediscovered doing trivial craft things together, like long-forgotten colouring books and knitting kits. We started singing badly and happily.

We had sex much more often than before—but its nature had now changed. It was faster, more breathless, strikingly shorter in duration, as if we were impelled by an animalistic urgency. It would pop up here and there during the day or night, effortless indulgence, urgent satisfaction of a common need, no preparation, no special journeys to our little boudoir, without either of us pausing to sense the mood of the other, safe in the knowledge that it was as quotidian and necessary as sleeping and eating. Perhaps in this way the act itself had lost its uniqueness, but its proliferation lent our relationship a uniqueness we had never experienced before. Our time was populated with one another in an almost total way.

Our newly found togetherness was enough not only to keep us folded in a close embrace with each other, but also to make us feel somehow angular and ill-fitting when it came to our contact with the others. All of a sudden we did not know how to stand when talking to Selina along the corridor or at the roof tap. Our bodies felt too unbending to negotiate Lorna's and Marek's low-lying branches and their well meaning chat.

Never in the past had we felt like exploring. But now we were following a different urge, a preparation. We started with our own building. We first searched the lower floors we had been ignoring all this time because of their lack of activity and people, and we progressively moved up to flats that had only recently been abandoned. We quickly became brasher and even a bit thuggish, breaking down obstinate doors, knocking down obstacles, chasing away persistent birds that had taken over. Once inside the various apartments, we would play games, trying out new household configurations, pretending that we were the people we imagined used to occupy these homes. At times we felt like archaeologists of human presences, wrapped up in a mania for experiencing and cataloguing the various emotions that we imagined the occupiers of the flats used to display. We would stage illicit trysts, outrageous dramas, newly wedded tenderness, in-laws visiting nightmares, love scenes of cinematic passion, clichés of shouting and throwing left-over vases and plates in mock ire. Our recreation of those domestic scenes was our way of embodying a long-lost otherness, experiencing it first-hand and allowing it to leave its trace in us.

Our own selves were expanding with every imaginary character we impersonated. We were taking in earnest to this new-found multiplicity. Especially when, during the games, the acting receded and gave rise to something uncanny—familiar but faraway. Those were the times when we knew something sensitive had been touched, something hiding on the edge of our fears and desires. Instead of giving up, we would persevere. We would stay longer in whichever flat it was, trying to recreate the supposed situation as faithfully as we could. We were following an imaginary script to its fullest development. Sometimes we would even spend the night in those peculiar atmospheres, away from the usual refuge of our own home. The newly discovered intensity of our intimacy emboldened us. We were carrying our nest between us wherever we were—the apartment being just a prop we could do without in our enlightened state of emotional minimalism.

The abandoned apartments were a treasure trove of experiences. Surrounded by all those things that people had had to leave behind—lifelong or even generations-old collections of belongings, displayed in such a way as to make their owner feel at home and their visitors in awe; precious materials of increasing fragility and irrelevance; lustred surfaces that had succumbed to the dampness of the new planet—all these were funny, bitter, empty, and instructive in equal measure. We would admire their beauty, often recalling things we had forgotten about: originality, value, preciousness, rarity. We would play pricing games in old money or in current commodities, often realising that we would not offer a single vegetable or bowl of rice in exchange for these goods.

These were exercises in shedding. Our bodies performed them without our realising. We were shedding our own dry, human, individual selves, and exposing our new and inexperienced skins to an atmosphere we could no longer control. We now know that this shedding had begun earlier. That night at the hospital—remember?—when Marek took us back home, when your breathing was hard and grating, mine panicking and shallow. The boat was rocking wildly on the water. We were all worried; we felt abandoned, really, perhaps for the first time with such a desperate intensity; and just at that point, Marek's natural calmness finally covered us like soft blue powder, and our breath, all our breaths, became one, a movement shared with the city.

Since then, a different sense of self had hesitantly emerged. This self was neither alone nor marked by individual boundaries. It was open, in some ways loose and multiple: it was as if it included an unbounded collectivity. Our aquatic horizon seemed to have moved past our retina and deeper into our sense of self.

At its core remained our own intimate togetherness. This togetherness had long ago—perhaps before the waters—stopped feeling like a multiplicity and more like an extension, you my extension and I yours, a breath continuum, with air circulating between our apertures as if it were a single lithe trace of floating moisture. But around us, like lightning gathering on a rod, there were others. Marek first, and then Luz and Olalekan, and recently Cinder and Toby. A community of sorts: fragmented, inoperable, lost, and unconnected but for the commonality of breathing that emerged when our bodies were close to one another.

Or earlier on in our new common lives, when we felt that our door should stay open to passing strangers; or even earlier than all this, when we started using the garden store as a space of primordial togetherness. Or even before that, quite early on, when we started shedding some of our senses and giving priority to smelling that which was air-bound, sniffing others out before we could even see them. Initially all this openness and commonality seemed like nostalgia, especially this gawky hanging on to the olfactory as if it were a wooden plank.

But we now know that we were shedding a side of our human nature.

The shed pile was growing: our initial attachment to the flat, our limited perambulations within the building, our fascination with and residual longing for material belongings, our unconscious holding onto bourgeois values, our challenged but still palpable sense of property, and above all our deep need for verticality: all these were slowly piling up, and we stood around observing them with increasing indifference and occasionally with ecstatic joy as we shed them. We were drunk on the possibilities of our bodies' movement—unfettered, svelte, differently connected. We were dizzy with the new primacy of the olfactory, as our noses quickly became as important as our ears. Perhaps for the first time in centuries we were succumbing as a species to a natural rather than a technological evolution. Or was it a regression? Whatever it was, it was all part of a trajectory, of an impetus towards somewhere. We experienced it like a horizon opening, a flatness to be explored, a depth to be fathomed, and a density to measure ourselves against.

### ten

Once we had exhausted our building, we started venturing to the neighbouring ones, only to find that they were even more deserted than ours. Fewer residents meant darker passages, more overgrown corridors, and deeper secrets behind their walls. The buildings were also more ravaged than ours. Not just because of the lack of maintenance, though there was that too, of course. In some cases we had to deal with collapsed staircases or gaping floors, with cavernous openings that let the sky in, or with unplanned atriums that tore the building from within. Some places were so violently stripped of anything of interest that they looked as if hordes of collectors had rummaged furiously before us.

The most devastating traces were those of human violence. The floors were littered with decomposing corpses of people who had clearly been killed in some conflict—victims perhaps of random attacks or of fights that had only ended at the point of death. There were bodies that looked half-eaten, blood streaks on murky carpets, traces of fights on the walls and furniture, screams suspended in mid-air in darkened rooms. Our skins became thin membranes that failed to exclude this influx of sadness and misery from our bodies. The intensity of our encounters with death and violence was so absolute that, perhaps for the first time, we accepted that the demise of humanity had arrived. The venom and beauty of the human presence, that overdetermining anthropic face of the planet, had plunged irreversibly into a self-destructive whirlpool. There was no surprise there. In the past we had all watched disaster movies and now we were re-enacting them, following the banality of their scripts to the letter. We were playing ourselves acting out our extinction.

On the other hand, every encounter with this violence reminded us of how grateful we were for our having somehow, miraculously, kept all this conflict at bay in our building. We often marvelled at our luck at having avoided those who wanted to loot, expand territorially, or kill for the fun of it. No doubt Marek's large metal hatch doors assisted in this regard, and must have worked as a deterrent to the passing looters. Perhaps the kind of violence that was ravaging outside our brittle bubble was so random, so thoughtless and unplanned, so desperate and objectless, that even a couple of metal doors were enough to deflect it to a nearby, easier, softer target.

As for the lack of violence amongst us, the shelter we had created in the shop and in our common spaces obviously succeeded in insulating us even from the fear of the other, from the horror that was taking place outside, especially during those early periods when people were leaving the city en masse. Stories that people had told us were now slowly re-emerging from that part of our memory that had been erased as soon as those horrors were deposited within it.

We were also defended by our very own mechanisms of forgetting and moving on. As if under the influence of some psychotropic drug, we were lulled into overlooking that side of human nature, our own otherness. The somnambulism of vegetal negotiations that took place in the garden shop kept us in a state of naïvete, blind to the raging outside. The network of hesitant mutual support that had emerged organically among us was our main depository of empathy. We had to block out the rest of the world and its plague.

Of course, those other buildings we were exploring during that period were harrowing reminders not just of a narrowly escaped past but of ever-present threats. The fear of collapse had never left us. But somehow, by creating our own cacophony of creepy creaking, foot-stamping thuds, and door-crashing commotion, we pushed the other noises away. We stopped listening to the way the buildings groaned and the cracks on the walls gushed. No longer an augury of future collapse, the various noises had been demoted to white noise surrounding our expeditions. Our pseudo-scientific approach, our sense of urgency, and our desire to accumulate emotions, maybe even the pride we felt when sharing our exploration stories with our neighbours and friends—all this endowed us with an inebriating bravado. We were blind to the risks and scares, placing an inordinate amount of trust in our ever-keener sense of smell and our meagre tools, such as a lamp and a couple of rods that we used to push things out of the way.

In retrospect, I think we were just tremendously lucky. Especially that one time, in that building in the same block as ours, directly opposite us. Just like ours, its rear overlooked what used to be the backyard of some college or other. It was a relatively underused space, hosting the occasional event that always finished early, and the rest of the time a cement stretch of relative nothingness.

We walked in this dark flat, which had three huge windows through which we could see not only the back side of our building but also our very own flat, or at least the rear side of it. The water surface separating us from our bedroom was calm, reflecting the daylight and sending it almost directly towards our bedroom. We could see our unmade bed, the wardrobe, even the books piled by your side of the bed.

You stood against the window looking out, imagining what the people here might have seen of us over the years. You started acting, an invitation to play: oh look, here they are again, going about their boring stuff, I wish we had some more exciting people living opposite, some action. I joined in: but they seem happy, content at least, or is this just a facade do you think? There might be a lurking melancholy that binds these two together, a fear of reality; and you said, they are certainly not afraid of us, look they never draw their curtains; but, I said, perhaps we do not count for them, we are not reality, they are not afraid of us, they are just indifferent to us, I am talking about another fear. "What fear?", you ask. Fear of dying, or fear of getting ill? These are always the standard culprits, no? No, I say, a different fear, I think; or perhaps not a fear, perhaps 'awe' is the right word. They are in awe of something, yet they seem to float well onto it. Look how strangely they move, as if swimming in their own flat. You were about to laugh this off and say something humorous and dry when, behind us, there was an animal scream, an empty thud, steps running towards us pulling along a broken floor lamp with a force that seemed impossible for such a reduced, emaciated human being; no human smell anymore but just a featureless fleshy sponge, at one with the background, a vessel brimming with despair, hurling his body towards us, the floor lamp held like a battering ram. I shout and push you out of the way, opening between us the full view of our flat, of a little piece of the water that had covered the block's inner courtyard, and a generous piece of cloudless sky—all that just a thin sliver of glass away, an invitation to a voyage this man accepted using us as a pretext, attack them! Do not attack yourself! But, really, he was the only target of his own hurling. His battering ram, smashing into flashing shards, was the only thing that could have stopped him, and it failed. His body dived on an arch of misery and into the waters below, with a cry echoing so much that it carried on even from underwater.

We were paralysed. We could not even bring ourselves to look down into the flooded courtyard. I eventually managed to stick my head out, careful not to cut myself on the broken glass pane, but I couldn't see a thing. Did he survive the fall? Was he trying to kill us, or were we the random but ultimately necessary witnesses to his suicide?

After the initial shock, a sense of affinity with him overwhelmed us: who was he, who did he used to be, why was he alone, how long had he been in that abandoned building, why did he jump, why now? All these questions that could have applied to so many others. So many facile answers that one could offer in order to close the matter off. Yet this time the questions posed themselves as if screamed from the man's drowning throat. The hollowness of any possible answer was intolerable.

There was something else too: that was the first and only time we tried to include ourselves in the play.

We were trying to perform an out-of-body experience: us looking at us. Us as subjects and objects at the same time. That splitting of I and me, of you-observer and you-observed, of we-actors and us-props. It could have led us to some unbearably seductive wormhole. It could have absorbed us even deeper into our little selves.

And then he darted between us, ripping our narcissism apart, showing us how self-indulgent we were, how enclosed in our own smug bubble.

Our sense of self was violently but inexorably changing.

### eleven

We developed a little routine during those early exploring days: start early and take breakfast with us. Take one building at a time, first the odd numbers, then the even ones. Focus on one floor at a time. Start from the top floors and make our way down.

A brief social moment also formed part of our routine. Before embarking on our daily adventures, we always greeted the old woman on the boat just outside our building. The boat was safely moored and she seemed to have no intention of moving it. We never had to seek her out. A strange thing this: she seemed almost to be waiting for us every time we ventured out, as if she knew. We never exchanged a word. She never really encouraged it. But she always nodded at us first. And we always nodded back, half-embarrassed and half-pleased that she had become part of a harmless ritual harking back to the old normality of social contact with strangers.

But after a few weeks of exploration, we finally arrived at what seemed like the end of the walkable plankways near our building. We had searched everything within the perimeter that the planks allowed us to access, which was not that much. Most of the network had collapsed or was about to do so because of the spreading rot. The will to maintain what had once been a genuinely busy and functioning web of connections had long since evaporated. The few planks still standing strong felt more like a hopeless gesture against eternity than a truly functional piece of engineering.

So perhaps this was finally the sign we had been waiting for—the sign that we should try further afield. Ever since we had started, a building had kept on popping up in my thoughts with a force I could not ignore. It would emerge from within the waters of my memory when I was brushing my teeth or re-arranging stuff in the flat or cleaning the bathroom: mindless activities that opened up geographies of unexpected desire and nostalgia. The building was important to us. There was no doubt that it was beautiful—a grand hotel with art deco features and, I remember, an impressive marble entrance that rose into an atrium filled with palm trees. But its beauty was not the reason I so wanted to visit it now. In the past, long before the waters, there used to be a café on the ground floor. That was the café of our very first rendezvous. At a table overlooking the street we had had our first contact with each other. We never went back to it after that rainy day. We always want-ed to, of course, but it eventually shut down. By that time the building had lost its magic for us, and we never felt the need to walk in.

Except for now. The desire was not about recon-structing our past but about understanding a part of our past that had always felt slightly murky. That was the part of our story that included the water even before the waters arrived. I remember our meeting as being already—how can I put it—aquatic, as if seen through water goggles, all bubbles and diffrac-tion. The café appears in my memory lying at the bottom of a well, with water filling up to the well's lip, light coming through the opening of the atrium above, palm trees freely floating about in a miracu-lous verticality, and the two of us centred, embraced by our embarrassment, pressed closer to each other under the pressure of vast volumes of slow water. I know it could not have been like that, but it seemed so natural by today's standards, so absolutely normal to meet in a café in the deep water, that my memory was allowed to be happily flooded.

I've always felt, albeit not without some hesitation, that the water we had first invited to nestle between us during our date could not have been the water that flooded the world only a few years later. Despite all assurances to the contrary, we—or was it just me—were still nursing the hope that these two waters were different. Not only that, but I was sure there was an undefinable number of other waters that had affected our love in a different way every time. The random-ness and effervescence of that first, intimate water of our courtship had little to do with the glaciality of the fixed wave that brought us together after Positano, which in turn had nothing to do with the stagnant water of our aquarium, filled with plants and blood.

Perhaps for one last, desperate time, I still needed to believe in other waters.

A return to the place of our first encounter, I hoped, would show us how things had changed. I would final-ly get some evidence to support my desperate hope. I wanted us to see, I wanted to show you—I don't know why I felt that you were not with me on this one, why I needed to prove to you that what I wanted to be-lieve was true, but I was feeling this urge speeding through my body. I needed us finally to see how that first water, sparkling with youthful brilliance, could still survive amidst the pool of the wet new world.

But there was no way to reach it on foot. It lay on the other side of town, in the old theatre area. It was only at times like this that I felt the pressing need for us to have a boat. We never wanted to own one. In the past, we had always relied on others to take us where we needed to go. We hardly ever ventured out without the excuse of an invitation and the borrowed facility of a boat. To own a boat would have felt a bit like a betrayal, at once a giving up and a giving in.

Floating artificially seemed like a way of relinquishing the hope of a dry world and accepting our own human limitations. Relying on others' boats felt like an acceptable concession.

### twelve

And so I jumped at the opportunity that late afternoon, when Luz and Olalekan suggested we go out on the dinghy for a trip around the old theatre area.

These two had now become an integral part of our everyday. Whatever we could not deal with directly, we allowed it to sink into the spaces between us, a sedimentation that we managed to ignore when the four of us were together. A huddling together against the outside. Our friendship had recently been further strengthened when they decided to move to our building. A reasonably well-maintained top floor flat had just become vacant, after the residents moved to what had once been a rather grand private members club nearby—no doubt in pursuit of some more comfortable old-world lodgings. Moves like this were becoming less and less frequent. Whoever wanted to move had already done so, and the ones who stayed put were those like us, floating in a familiar yet immobilising and slightly anaesthetising bubble. So when we found out about the flat, we immediately told Luz and Olalekan, in the hope that they would become a more intimate part of our day-to-day life. And so they did.

Their new flat was bare and luminous, inviting in an uninterrupted view of the flooded city. Their moving in was unfussed: they appeared as if for a casual visit. They brought with them only two large canvas bags that contained all of their possessions, plus the clothes they were wearing. They set up their home the same day, sleeping on a found mattress and spending their days on soft rugs spread around the living room. The only objects, apart from clothes and boat accessories, that they brought along from their previous place were a few books and Luz's flute.

She was not particularly good at playing it, but in a world deprived of music, anything was welcome. Her practising sometimes served as a summons for those nearby to pop in for some companionship and musical improvisation. We progressively learned to relax with only a few musical notes, which soothed us by virtue of their endless, meditative repetition.

Soon after we started using their dinghy more and more, but we never ventured far. Only short journeys to pick up material, or perhaps for the occasional dusk ride to admire the waterways. One day when we were all sitting together talking idly, I dropped the idea of a trip further afield to revisit the old café, but Luz said that there was no point. She had recently heard that the building had collapsed.

We all clouded over. To me it was a loss of vital proof of our last vestige of verticality, our ultimate differentiation from the waters, however inane that might sound. That hotel had felt to me like the last piece of memory linking me to an intimate and important part of my past, and it had taken on a disproportionate weight. To Olalekan the news seemed to have an even deeper effect. Luz told us that, apparently, the few people who had moved into the building were all killed in the collapse. None of us really had any personal connection to them, and our automatic reaction was to consider ourselves lucky to still be alive in a building that was still standing. We did not say it though, not in front of Olalekan. In a slightly irritated and curt way he said that he was adamant the building was still there. You asked him whether he had recently been in the area, but he did not respond. He just repeated, mantra-like and somewhat incongruously, it is still there. The collapse of the tower echoed in every rumour about other collapses, plunging Olalekan into a perpetually repeating trauma from which he could not recover.

The mood was heavy, but we still decided to set out. The afternoon was dazzling, with an autumn sun sending its horizontal rays across the waters. It started as an innocent observation along the lines of "wasn't there a building here?", and then it quickly became a strange game: spotting gaps in the urban fabric and debating whether there had been buildings standing there. The whole city became as distant as a video game, with our mnemonic avatars vying to convince each other that there had once been buildings where only a quiet flatness could now be observed.

My fear of never seeing the café again was subsiding: it's OK, it is a sign, we need to move on. Even Olalekan's mood was improving through our unexpected, homeopathic way of making light of our trauma. As the day progressed, he participated earnestly in this exercise in cruelty as if his previous heaviness had nothing to do with it. As if we still had a few lives left in this round of our video game. We were all becoming progressively desensitised to the tragedies behind the gaps, even reaching the point of knowingly fabulating—oh yeah of course, don't you remember, there was that ten-storey office building here with the funny awnings—or sometimes simply exaggerating the features, erecting baroque turrets and neoclassical facades where only carparks or unassuming squares had once been. How about that bright pink residential building right here where the water is lapping into a whirlpool circling nothing but itself; massive building, silver grey with that wavy pattern on its windows. The more enthusiastic we were, the better it served to convince the others, so that we could be the first ones to spot a gap and score another pointless point. We took a perverse pleasure in identifying sites of potential disaster around us, gleefully basking in our good fortune at remaining alive with a roof over our heads.

For a while we carried on playing that game quite unapologetically, loud kids spotting red cars, brazenly and excitedly, forgetting that in our real lives we were falling asleep and waking up with our own collapse in mind. But then we reached that eery area between the business zone and the theatre district—strange even during dry times, with a series of low residential buildings, unkempt parks, and a series of parking lots. This transit zone had always suffered from a lack of character; dry and dull, not even functional, just a thing to get through. It was always being proposed for redevelopment, but nothing had ever happened. It was now completely submerged, almost a separate laguna, with nothing of note breaking the flatness. There was nothing for us to spot and no convincing way of pretending that we had indeed spotted something that had once stood. We took a notional diagonal that traversed the area, the quickest possible way out of there. It was an area unmoored from either memories or future collapses, already deep in a collapse that had left nothing behind. We fell silent.

### thirteen

It was early evening when we finally reached the theatre district. What had once been a short, five-minute metro ride was a question of patient rowing for a good half hour. The previously buzzing streets of entertainment halls and restaurants now lay below mossy theatre roofs like baroque replicas of ships forever moored, forever soaking. We were surrounded by still-standing poles from old cultural institutions on which coloured drapes announcing current and future events had once fluttered—now replaced by long, lank weeds. We sailed past the top part of a multiplex whose upper floors and roof terrace were filled with broken pieces of wood and torn items of clothing that flapped in the wind like Buddhist flags. We even spotted the old opera dome in the distance, catching the sun on what remained of its old gilt, attracting us like a floating bollard. We changed our route just to get close to it. It felt like a crown on a beheaded sovereign, barely balancing atop his rolled skull. We came close enough to reach out to its mossy surface. Just as we touched the metal surface with our fingers, perilously balancing between the rocking dinghy and the slippery dome surface, a vertigo overcame us, as if we had only just noticed the volumes of water right under our feet, the open mouths waiting to swallow us along the flow.

The area had retained a grandeur and even a buzz, despite the fact that it was now almost totally abandoned. The buzz was no longer a human one. The open interior spaces of the theatres, with their echoing roofs and their long horizontal beams where the set ropes used to hang, had become the perfect refuge for vast colonies of birds. The caws, whistles, and cries pouring out of these majestic loudspeakers sounded distant and yet vivid, as if reaching us from another continent. We didn't encounter a single human in any of the buildings in the surrounding area. It was abundantly clear who the new chiefs of the theatre district were.

Luz was the first to spot the hotel. It was still standing! We burst in ululations of wild joy, like hunters spotting their prey. As we were approaching, though, we started noticing some odd things. We remembered it being flanked by buildings on either side, at least as tall, if not taller. Standing there on its own, it looked naked, somehow abandoned. Was that our memory playing tricks on, us or had actual collapses taken place? The sense of isolation and disconnectedness was accentuated by the fact that the whole building looked slightly lopsided, as if announcing its imminent collapse.

We tied up the dinghy and climbed into the cool dimness of the floor just above the building's art deco arched facade. It must have been the hotel's breakfast area or some other large function room, an open mezzanine now devoid of furniture. Its central section was taken up by the elaborate top end of the grand marble staircase that we all remembered. The staircase led to the atrium below, now entirely under water. No signs of human presence could be seen. We listened out for anything like movement coming from above, but we could hear nothing. We

walked gingerly, the sense of trespassing more potent than the mores of the flooded city would usually
have dictated, each of us separate and in some way
disconnected from the rest of the group. After a good
walk about, Olalekan and Luz climbed the stairs to
the floors above in search of other distractions. The
ceiling soon started vibrating with their giggles and
rapid runs across the corridors.

Neither of us wanted to go upstairs. Our goal was
to try and take a good look, from as near as possible, at the atrium café downstairs. I walked to the
staircase and stood on the precipice, at the top of the
staircase leading to the vast atrium space. The whole
interior beneath my feet was gently rocking with the
lapping waters. Tentacled vegetation had taken over
the space. A shaft of evening sunlight was refracted
through the sunken facade, shedding some light on
the space and making it look like the salon of a sub-
marine—opulent but fake, paper-thin, as if haphaz-
ardly constructed by a film crew.

The steps seemed solid, promisingly extending
deep in the atrium's thick green. I imagined that I
could start walking down the steps one by one and
carry on walking without losing my upright posture,
without even needing to hold onto the majestic curvature of the handrail. I would make a grand entrance to that oceanic world of our past. You walked
towards me and, taking a bow, motioned me theatri-
cally towards the steps, as if you had read my mind. I
took a hesitant first step, dipping my foot just below
the surface of the water. The marble steps were slippery. An image came to my mind.

The sharp glint of a guillotine before it nosedives.

You followed and reached for my hand. We then
took a step—propping each other up—playfully but
in silence. And then another. We were moving slowly, in ceremony, announced by the fanfare of an
imaginary orchestra. It was all becoming a bit of
a struggle, though: the steps were treacherous and
the water was pushing us upwards, making it hard

to stay standing. We were already half submerged, and while I was preparing for yet another step, you gently dipped, sat on the step, and softly pulled me down next to you. The water was now coming up to the middle of our faces. With a bit of an effort we could keep it between upper lips and noses, those leaking points on our faces already accustomed to the humidity of exhalations, mucus, and saliva. We sat there, not talking, our scant breathing slowly opening to the rhythm of the building and eventually falling into synchrony with the mild lapping of the water contained by the walls. Our heartbeats were resonating with the space around us.

And then I placed my palms on the step where we were sitting and let my body slide down, just one step below but enough for the water to cover me completely. As soon as my head went under, my eyes suddenly faced the viscosity of the water as if for the first time. My nostrils filled with impossibility. My first instinct was to come out of that thick infestation, where breath was lacking, space constricting, infection advancing. Yet I resisted. I stayed, not breathing, not even wanting to think about breathing, ignoring the feeling of suffocation rising within me. I felt you move next to me.

We rested there for a while, at peace, as if we had finally found our place, or as if *we had found ourselves* in that place: *on se trouve, ci si trova, wir uns befinden*. That odd grammatical construction where one encounters one's very own pronoun, a perfect mirroring of self and self, the seamless tautology of identity.

We found ourselves in other grammars.

But this pause could not last. It was as if it desired more from us, whatever that 'it' was, wherever it came from. One thing was certain: that 'it' was not the water we knew. Nor was it the city, or the future, or even the past. It was something else, altogether vaster, uncontainable, unthinkable. Whatever it was, it was crying out in our blocked ears: Move! Carry on! This is not enough! And at that point, two choices opened up: either an easy press up back to the dry, to the air above—a space of openness and life but also a space that at that moment felt somehow weak, sparse, scantily populated—or a sliding further down, deeper into the water, into a daunting but seductive density that we knew we could never negotiate.

And just like that, we let go.

We lifted our arms, unclenched our bodies, and surrendered our breaths. But instead of being pushed up, emerging like garlanded Ophelias floating on their wet graves, we were pulled downwards. Who was pulling us? Was it us? Was it the water? Was it our past, craving to be rediscovered? Was it that mysterious 'it' we could both feel but could not recognise as anything we had encountered so far?

The waters whirled around us like colossal suckers, pulling us down below, into the dark water volumes of the overgrown atrium. We precipitated down the verticality of the gilded glass facade, scratching against the stained glass and the liquiferous branches. We finally reached the ground floor perching on the savagely proliferating flora. Two lovers-to-be, first me then you, entering separately the space of their past meeting, sliding in the hope of connection, buoyed by the desire for this to work and at the same time slowed down by the weight of past failures, both of us assuming our place for the grand re-enactment, me first, waiting for the one I have never met, then you, looking for the one you have never met, our nevers doing a little dance of heavenly nuptials in the middle of the vast atrium filled with light and expectation.

I was running out of breath. With what seemed like a preterhuman effort, I managed to come up to the surface. I broke the water, my eyes looking up to the glass dome of the building, half-blinded by the metallic yellow light that was pouring in. The dome was almost intact, with just a few holes symmetrically scattered around its flanks, making the place look like an Ottoman bathhouse whose waters had run amok and gurgled up to the ceiling. You popped up straight after me, your face transformed by a wild smile, by childlike impatience and joy at the adventure. Hello, I say. Hi! you exclaim, a little too enthusiastically. Nice to meet you, I say, really nice, you say, and what a great suggestion to meet here. Have you never been? No never, my first time, oh yeah it's a great place and the coffee isn't bad at all, oh good I'd love a coffee may I get you something too? No, it's OK, I can come along, no, no stay I'll get it, what would you like, an espresso please, OK, anything to nibble on, oh OK, yeah, why not, something chocolatey perhaps? Sure, I'll be back in a moment, oh and, yes, a bottle of sparkling water please, sure, I'll get us a large one to share, great, thanks. A fizzy whirlwind of words, air on the surface of our past, flutterings above the waters, other worlds, same words, the past that blossoms in bursting bubbles of aerated expectation; here we are again.

I dived again, nodding you to follow. My mission was to find the table of our first meeting. My mission was to find our own water. I needed to believe in a better world, a world outside this one. I needed to drag from the mud of the past a round bubble of fresh, unspoiled water. I still believed in innocence regained. But that was going to be the last time.

We knew of course we would not find a table or even the café. We were already swimming in something else. An amniotic fluid that was rushing in from the past and into our present was holding us up and hugging us in, enclosing us in a vision of other universes. We did not mind that the palm trees had become scaffolding for vast aquatic climbers, or that the marble floors and walls had become partitions of an infested swimming pool, a rusting testament to an asphyxiating infinity. We were looking for our table, hands busy with the tray, coffees and chocolate brownies and that bottle of water perilously balancing amidst the waves of the atrium, going down towards the window facade, swimming past volumes of breathlessness. To the left, the table is free, two chairs—or was it three?—one for the coats, rest the tray on the table, can you hold it please till I empty it, the water is heavy, I know, it is always such a struggle, thank you for this, no, I thank *you*.

You looked up, taking in the dome's refraction in the water, the wild overgrowth that was saturating the water with a deep green, the central chandelier still hanging from the massive beams yet somehow floating upside-down, creating another cupola. A dome within a dome, a double cupping presence delimiting our space in ever closer rounds, an aquarium enclosed by a much larger aquarium. The stillness of the submerged city was slowly flowing past us, against the surprisingly resilient glass facade that still separated us from out there. So many different waters, such impossibly thin differentiations.

You asked, "shall I pour?" Please, yes thanks, I say, lifting my glass and offering its emptiness to the aeriated flow. You picked up the water bottle and started pouring, just like then, ready to pour enough water into my glass for me to knock it later on and for us to start tracing little lines of destiny on the surface of the table. Left to right, left to right, underlining or inviting, from the tips of our fingers a zillion yesses blooming.

A constellation of conduits was channelled between us, and our distance became water

Of course, there was no table. There was nothing. There was just a pool made of thick past and trembling nostalgia. There was us there, but we were no longer the ones we had once been. Not in the usual sense of time passing, of growing older, of life's changes. That too, of course. But mainly in the sense that our bodies and minds had been diluted by that irrepressible influx of water. It was the first time that we traced that arched bridge between then and now in an attempt to link this side of the water with that. Something had cracked open, a different biology that was sprouting from our pores and harking ahead to a flat aquatic surface future. We were different now.

We now seemed to learn how to enter the water.

But we did not know how to pour. For that, we need-ed an emptiness that was nowhere to be found in this world. I lifted my glass and you leaned the bottle to-wards it. We made all the right moves. But nothing came out that wasn't already there. Water everywhere, flooding then and flooding now. The glass, the ges-tures, the café, the atrium: already filled. I realised, not for the first time but now finally resigned to it: we have always been here.

There it was again, that feeling of being watched by ourselves from afar—this time, however, not from a different space but from a different time. The same disembodied feel, the same sensation of violation as when we looked into our bedroom window from the building facing ours. Except that, this time, the eruption of violence did not come from a stranger but from deep within our consciousness: the finality of the realisation that there had only ever been one water made the immanence of this world asphyxiat-ing but also redeeming.

The table evaporated. The past receded. Your hand glided away from mine. We drifted apart. You some-where else, me somewhere here, floating mid-wa-ter in that gigantic baptismal urn, resigned to our ever-departing past.

I looked for you but the water had taken you across the atrium, suspended mid-water. Your eyes were shut, you looked as if you were in a trance. I wanted to communicate with you—I don't know, touch you, hold onto you, even just look at you meaningfully— but I could not. I kept looking at you, hoping that you would open your eyes. You kept them shut, al-though I was sure that you knew I was looking at you. I could not find you. Your closed eyes were a differ-ent universe, a parallel big bang whose reverberation would reach me aeons later. Don't get me wrong, you were you, you were yourself throughout this, you were there with me. Even your closed eyes were consistent with what I knew and loved about you. But you were also beyond reach. Our connection was mediated by something much bigger than either of us. It was as if we had found something that was the other for each other, a floating calm that sheltered us from harshness, a refuge of breathlessness. I let my eyes close too, finding a drop of breath within myself and spreading it through my body.

Our watery existence, our love and desire, have always been nestled deep in our planet's infinity pool—one immense aquatic sameness traversed by waterlines on their way to the rest of the universe. There was nothing to hold us anymore. We were thrown in there, small fish swimming within a school of gigantic divinities. It seemed that we were finally, finally, allowed to join our deepest desires, those Sirens of the flooded city bathing and whispering in pulmonic consonants their invitation to a voyage without return. It was not easy. We found ourselves right in the middle of a cosmic velocity, much faster and more brutal than anything we had experienced so far. We were pushed and pulled by what felt like an invisible crowd, translucent bodies whose contours were barely discernible, heavenly bodies that ignored us, shoving us aside and in the process making us spin around ourselves like dying goldfish.

But despite the violence of that pull, it felt like a return.

For a brief moment, we became part of a multiplicity, one drop among thousands of oceans, one breath exhaled in the aether—but we had finally, however briefly, however temporarily, however perhaps randomly, stopped being mere observers. We had become *part* of it. The violence was pure, the thrust primordial, the speed terrifying, and even our separation from each other felt complete and almost final. But in losing each other in the water, we found a different each other. Perhaps for the first time, we really found each other.

We were dying a new life.

## fourteen

Olalekan was standing above me screaming something far too loudly. It sounded more like a series of
vowels than actual words. I felt a peculiar dryness
sticking to my skin, like a desert wind pumicing me
with sand. I sat up and saw you lying down, your
eyes shut. It all came back like a syncopated breath.
In panic I threw myself towards you but failed and
collapsed on my back almost immediately. Luz was
with you, trying to bring you back to consciousness, shouting things as incomprehensible as what
Olalekan had been shouting at me moments before.
I was so worried about you that I started fighting
against Olalekan's arms, thinking that he was trying
to hold me back when he was only trying to prevent
me from collapsing yet again. I finally realised that
he was helping me towards you.

You were only a few feet away, but the distance felt
vast. When we got to you, your eyebrows were moving as if you were desperately trying to open your
eyes but something was keeping them locked. Luz
was shouting even louder now, probably encouraging you to come to, and it was working because you
were turning your head towards her voice. I threw
myself alongside your body, holding your hands in
my hands and saying again and again the only words
I could say at that moment, the only words that felt
right: I kept saying,

I am sorry.

Luz had come down earlier to fetch us upstairs.
They had found an oddly solid balcony overlooking
the district and had even managed to come across a
still stocked minibar—perfect for a sundowner before making our way back across the city. She tried
to find us to share the drink but couldn't find us anywhere. Olalekan eventually joined her, only to find
her looking intensely into the water and saying, can
you see something there, is that them, is that a body,
what is it?

The night was falling and the hotel was slowly dipping into a wet dusk, making it all much harder. Olalekan rushed out to the dinghy and brought in the oil lamp. He lit it and stepped onto the upper steps of the staircase, trying not to slip, stretching the light as far away from his body as he could, desperately squinting against the bright lamp and the deep green of the water.

And they saw us in that vast aquarium, suspended half-way between the floor and the water surface, circling the grand marble staircase. We were immobile but spread out, starfish under the sun, fingers like tentacles and toes like anemones. We were floating far apart from each other but strangely in unison, same posture and same orientation, as if we were moving along the exact same current. They couldn't be sure but they felt we were still alive. There was a vital tension in us, apparently different to a rigor mortis. Still, we looked too bizarre to be alive.

Luz jumped in while Olalekan held the light. She pulled me out first and then jumped back in again for you. You had moved closer to the staircase while she was pulling me out, as if you were following me. She pretty much threw me onto the floor, entrusting me to Olalekan's care. She did not wait to take a good look at me. If she had, she would have seen that my eyes were still open. Olalekan was alarmed by what he later described as a glassy openness, frightened that I might be in some sort of freeze shock. But he started rubbing me and shaking me vigorously, shouting my name all along while Luz was pulling you out and doing the same. Your eyes were shut, almost obstinately turned inwards. It took longer for you to come to. It was as if you were resisting it, as if you were drawn back into that aquatic nest of safety and violence.

You never quite heard my whimpering apologies. By the time you regained full consciousness, I too had calmed down. I was not sure why I had been apologising in the first place. I felt as if it were my fault for dragging you in there and almost killing you. Something inside me was pulling me into that liquid suspension, and you just followed because you loved me. I felt as if my love for you would cost us your life. I was throwing onto you all my anxiety.

I was reverting to a way of thinking of us as separate.

It was safer that way, more familiar. I could still find a place for my guilt, my sense of responsibility. It was too much for me at that time, when we were made to think that we had nearly died, when we were made to feel that we had returned to the dry land of living by a pure stroke of luck; it was too much to accept what we had encountered in that water. It was too much to think of us as no longer separate but as one and yet dispersed in an element much vaster than even our grander thoughts.

But it was not as hard for you. When you felt stronger and calmer, you turned to me and said without drama, without emphasis, with an equanimous voice that was stating a fact, nothing more, you said,

I was you.

Perhaps even more than that, I thought. Perhaps, for a moment, we were it. But I did not say it. I did not know what we could do with it.

### fifteen

We were silent on our way back. The temperature had risen, a fleshy mist was hovering above the waters. Navigating was like walking into a treacherous sound-box. All the usual noises got multiplied and refracted, as if coming from different sides at the same time. Bird caws, water gurgles, the city's many creakings were now so diffused and loud, their echo so dry and flat through the sheets of mist, that we were all gripped by an irrational fear. We knew that nothing could serious-ly threaten us—most of the large mammals had died off, and we had yet to come across any dangerous sea species. Humans could always be a threat of sorts but, in that thick soup, it seemed unlikely that we would be spotted by anyone. Luz's steering competence had been proven again and again, and no one seriously doubted her ability to deal with the emerging shallows, or the various protruding poles and still-standing trees. She seemed to have an almost innate seafaring instinct, making us all feel safe.

No, we knew that our fear had no basis. Yet we also felt defenceless against it, and no one was really ready to talk about it. Our experience in the hotel had numbed us to the point of speechlessness. For Luz and Olalekan, having seen us the way they did, having fought for our lives in a way we seemingly hadn't, it was too alienating. Although it was never articulated, we could sense a distance growing between us and them. That limbo between life and death that we had briefly inhabited while floating in an almost wilful way must have felt to them like a betrayal. But we could do nothing to alleviate this impression. We were both too immersed in the memory of this new experience—new but also unbearably ancient. We had no language to explain it. More than that, we had no will to bridge that distance between us—we who had moved into something beyond us— and them, who were still frolicking on the surface.

It felt as if we were all finding a certain solace in the thickness that was closing in upon us. We were projecting our fears onto that vaporous wall as if it were an open-air cinema. Our emotional confusion resonated with our spatial confusion, and we had comfortably resigned ourselves to it. Olalekan finally ventured a question, something about who fell in first or who tried to save whom, all uttered lightly and carefully, as if he too was afraid of touching something that might suck him in. But even that threw us into a deeper confusion because, well, neither of us had done any of that. My initial shame and that engulfing need to apologise had been replaced by a lapping understanding that we were both in it together. Perhaps for the first time in my life I felt that you and I were a flock of birds, a school of stingrays—I don't know, something more than human anyway, moving in unison, no leader or follower, no predetermination, no decision, just bodies ushering their consciousness forward.

We had been crossing the old night district, a low-level high-density area which was now mostly submerged. The occasional surviving taller building breaking the surface was undetectable because of the mist, only becoming visible from within a few metres. We were just passing in front of one such building, an unusually tall nightclub several stories high that was already past its glory days when the waters came. We came so close to it that we could touch its external walls, a deep mossy green glistening in the overcast night light. But nobody touched them. You started answering Olalekan's queries in what felt like a compromising way. Let's bridge that distance. You were earnestly trying to explain how we took the steps together, just wanted to see how far we would go, you even started saying something about the water, but then, mid-sentence, syllable left hanging, you stopped abruptly, as if you had heard a sound. No, I am certain, there was a sound, I heard it too, what was it? From somewhere across the water, a whistle or something, but different, deeper, tellurian, a chthonic rattle, the planet turning, and with it you also turning and looking at me. I was careful not to express anything, just looked back at you, and then, as if just realising, you said, no it didn't happen like that, I have no idea what happened. But I knew differently then; I knew that you knew what had happened, even though you could not find the words for it.

### sixteen

The night was turning cold. Tiredness and sadness were evaporating from us, slowing us down. We finally reached home. There was hardly a noise around except for the gentle lapping of the waves against the dark facades. The neighbourhood's few remaining residents seemed to have retired for the night. Other than our boat's storm lamp, which was getting fainter by the minute, there was only one other pale light, diffused and otherworldly in the humidity, probably coming from a window a few buildings downstream.

The double hatched doors leading into our building were already shut. Marek had got into the habit of locking them earlier and earlier, and occasionally even left them locked for the whole day until someone wanted to go out or come in. We knocked on the echoing metal surface, waiting for him to come down and open. Marek was the only one who could handle the heavy doors unaided. He was normally quick, popping his head out of a window and waving, always happy to let us in, but this time he must have been somewhere deep in the building and we had to wait.

We stood there shivering, feeling overexposed to a wet distended present, pregnant with an irreversible past. We had withdrawn into coils of couplehood, Luz and Olalekan still in the dinghy, us on the planks in front of our gates. While trying to manage our impatience, we felt a gaze, as if someone was breathing down our backs. We turned and saw the old woman whose boat was still moored just outside our entrance, standing on the deck and looking at us. She had stepped out from her hatch on purpose. She had an expectant air about her, her body wrapped in a spaying severity. She looked at us from top to bottom, checking our wet clothes, our tangled hair, our skins paled with fatigue. We felt singled out, as if Luz and Olalekan were not there with us. The way she looked at us was as if she was looking into the mirror, a gaze cast by herself and to herself, yet to us. We felt dizzy with the implications of this: it was as if she and we were co-extensive, as if she was looking at us from the other end of the same self.

The world curled up from all sides, like a wave closing into itself.

We gasped for air. We started apologising for our coughing noises, a desperate attempt to diffuse the tension and break the spell. Our words were coming out flaccidly, falling in the water between the planks and the boat, never reaching across. She did not react to any of that. She just went on gazing. And then she finally said in a quiet, underground roar,

*are you ready then.*

It was not really a question. There was no question mark anywhere in the sentence, in her large mouth with her tellurian, dried-up lips, in her body posture unhinged and straight as if no water movement could ever affect her uprightness. There was no question mark in the air between her and us. There was no question mark breezing onto our faces from that wet urban dusk. Instead there was only one vertiginous affirmation.

And so she carried on: bring your water box. We are leaving tomorrow. What water box? You still have it, don't you. Again, no question mark. Just a long piercing gaze into our bodies, hovering over our palms and fingers for just a second, the memory of a smooth slick surface, a toy or a thing with which to spend time mindlessly, the thing moving straight into our living room, evening light falling across the bookcase between two books, which books were they? An object waiting. A long piercing gaze into our past—remember? That late night visitor who spent the night and fixed our shutter, what happened to him? An abrupt arrival and an even more abrupt departure, who was he? A deposit of gratitude on our table the following morning. A rectangular plastic box, transparent, half-filled with murky water.

Yes, we have it.

What water box? asked Luz standing up in the boat. What is it? The woman ignored her. We looked back and forth between them, an awkward triangulation, distance and common breath. Bring it, she said looking only at the two of us. What for? No, we did not ask. We did not even nod. We just stood there looking at her. Offended, threatened, fearful, but also vibrating inside with anticipation, with wave upon wave of expectation: finally, it is time.

At that very moment, a radiant smile spread on the woman's face, open and anointing like mother. Sleep well, she said—a different voice, a different person. She breathed with us, gently pushing her exhalation across like a tender hand on our face, meeting our breath and settling in there. Another end of self, even, yet still part of the same self. A rapid moebius strip flashing both its sides before our eyes, a whirlwind of identity and difference reaching a static but manic crescendo, and, right then, a squeaking noise above. Marek finally appeared at the window, hi there, will be down in a second.

### seventeen

The world changed gear. We hastily parted from Luz and Olalekan, shouting to them, quick, see you down there, bring the water box, quick. What water box, what are you all talking about? Olalekan said. The one that strange man left the night he visited the building, you remember, don't you? Anyway, it doesn't matter, maybe she was only talking about our box, quick. We rushed up to the flat and frantically started packing. We amassed an inordinate amount of clothes, things, foodstuff, books, cramming it all into the long-unused suitcases we had stored underneath our bed. The whole place turned febrile, flashing red, alarm and excitement, as if the walls were now kicking us out and even a single night longer in the flat would now be too much. Our bodies were tensed up like hunting animals, ready to pounce down the staircase and into the night.

We were running around, no longer picking up things to take with us but mentally bidding farewell to the various rooms, surfaces, and nooks. We realised that we were getting ready never to return. We were even working on whatever nostalgia we felt we might suffer from later on, taking mental snapshots of the flat and trying to shed whatever sense of belonging we felt. Despite our drenched exhaustion, we felt propelled into a readiness and urgency for escape of which we had never imagined ourselves capable.

Mid-run from the bedroom to the kitchen, you stopped and said, how about the others? Are we just going to leave without telling them? Sobering doubts poured down upon us. Were we really leaving? Did we understand the woman's intentions correctly? Are we mad, leaving with a woman we hardly know? The deep impression she had made on us earlier now seemed like a sleight of hand, a hypnotist's trick. What could she possibly want from us? And why just us? Even though Luz and Olalekan had been there, we felt that the invitation was directed almost exclusively to us. They were not excluded from it but their inclusion seemed ancillary. They were not the actual recipients of the summons. Mistrust and fear were tipping towards seeing the overstuffed suitcases as a pathetic attempt to hold on to whatever we could. This was bound to fail.

But it was already too late. During that brief running around, we had managed to denude the flat of every emotional appendage. It now felt draughty and humid, cold to the bone. This was all it took, apparently—this and the roaring accumulation of experiences that had elongated our bodies to the point of our breaking in the direction of an unknown horizon. We could not stay put. But we could extend a hand to the collectivity of which we were part. Fragmented and isolated, a community of absences rather than presences, a community of withdrawal rather than participation, yes, no doubt; but also, a community of undercurrent connections, of synchronised breaths and smells. The only community we had left.

We ought to have had more faith in this intangible communication. A knock on our door set us off in a new flurry of activity, this time even more inane and objectless, half-hiding stuff, half-assuming normality. When we calmed down and finally opened the door, we did not see the old woman as we initially feared. A thread of our diffused synchronicity was standing right at the door, an echo of our breathing. It was Marek saying, softly and tenderly but still resonant of that disarming affirmation that had showered us with trepidation and delight,

are you ready then.

Who is going? You asked. Everyone. We are meeting in an hour. Don't take too much with you, there is no room. Did you speak to the woman? I asked; no, said Marek, I spoke to Toby, it's all settled. But are we all leaving with the woman's boat? No, only you are. Everyone is taking their own boat. It will be a fleet! The joy was oozing from every syllable—a wild, frightening joy, a pulsating collectivity of desire, a common thought that was moving all bodies, human and nonhuman alike, towards an unknown goal.

You were still talking to Marek at the door, arranging details: how many containers can we find for water, how can we fill them all and carry them down. We will need all the food we can find—these were the priorities. I decided to run next door to Selina's and make sure that everyone was on board with water and food. Their door was ajar and the same amber frenzy was radiating from their flat, the same shouts and rushed darting across rooms to pick up stuff. I walked in, donning what I felt was an appropriately rushed and matter-of-fact attitude and hiding my nagging question. how had they also decided to make the move tonight? Did they get the same invitation? They greeted me with the same ecstatic joy as Marek had, and even the same sentence, although here it was much more high-pitched and clearly enunciated:

are you ready then.

Like an anthropologist on an expedition, I felt that I needed to pick up the salutational aspect of the sentence and reiterate it—an affirmation of commonality and togetherness that seemed to have replaced the usual hello.

Are you ready then.

I almost shouted. Cinder came over to give me a quick hug. Toby is coming too, right?, I asked; of course! he said. Please take with you as many water containers and as much food as you can. Already done, Cinder said. And then I asked, are you taking the water box; yes, yes, we know all about it, you wouldn't go abroad without your passport, would you, and he ran away, turning towards me and saying, don't forget yours.

I felt lost. I had no idea how they had all come to the same decision at the same time, and what the role of the water box had been. I was reluctant to start a more in-depth discussion about all this, and, anyway, no one seemed able to listen, even if I had had the temerity to broach the issue. I felt guilty because I thought that we had got a special invitation from the woman on the boat, which we had not thought of sharing until much later. And now we were joyfully ambushed by a common knowledge whose source of commonality eluded us. Guilt was replaced by worry and even disbelief: were they the ones that actually knew, perhaps even before us, and they never told us? There was something happening inside me, a beast growling, an awakening of a part of me I thought I had put to sleep some time ago. All too human of course, but still, these feelings of being left out, of not knowing, of feeling lost while in the middle of a vertiginous speed field in which the whole planet seemed to be turning faster, these feelings left me exhausted, sad, and aggressive. I did not know what to do. I came back home and started unpacking our suitcases, getting rid of stuff that I had previously considered indispensable.

Not enough shedding, I thought. More shedding needed.

You walked in and sat on the bed next to the open suitcase.

### eighteen

Are you alright, you asked. I had to sit down. My breath was scratching against something almost calcified, a grout wheezing in my upper lungs and throat. I was feeling distraught. The realisation that everyone seemed to know, and perhaps had known before we did, had a double effect. It made me feel that I was late to the party, excluded before being included. But it also made me realise that, in the midst of this cotton-wool community of ours, full of breaths and common rising, metal rods were hiding, making the whole thing a trap.

You tried to reason with me. You tried to show me how my fear was unfounded: how did I even know that they knew before we did? How did I reconcile the personal intensity of the summons from the old woman with the fear of being excluded? I could see that it did not make sense; I could see it, but it wasn't helping. It was as if this trace of rancour was what I needed in order to keep myself from finally leaving. As if I was making up the whole situation so as to justify my fear of fleeing.

You held my hands, looked into my eyes, and started breathing, encouraging me to breathe along with you: shared rasp and pooled hiss, breezes caressing the bodies in the room, our meteorologies expanding, slow wide breaths distending the walls and floor. Right at the top of that oxygen arc, at our most filled and exposed, we heard other breaths, same but different again: our building was synchronised,

one breath one arc one luminous edifice of opening.

We were zooming out, the whole building as one. We were zooming in, every thing breathing its own breath. A forensic breathing, a scanning of our extended body: from the waiting woman moored outside and the gently rocking boats tied to our architectural tentacles, up to the gates reverberating with our communion and preserving our fortress, then a bit further up to Marek's and Lorna's preservation of the overgrown jungle, sliding up to Cinder's and Toby's preservation of ludic dryness, whooshing up and in the process shedding all traces of nostalgia, breathing out our collective breath in staircases and corridors—no more preservation! breathe it out!—up to our floor, don't knock, all doors open and flapping with our breath, our rooms co-extensive with Selina's, then up to Toby's flat, into him through his feet and out again, higher towards Luz and Olalekan grounded up on the highest floor, and then finally plunging into the water of our rooftop tap and through that to the waters old and new around us and in us, and to the whole city trembling with anticipation at our readiness, a little pulsating blue spot on the surface of the planet.

We had become us.

## nineteen

We managed to get a brief, brittle sleep. Our bodies curled next to each other without bothering to go under the duvet, sharing bed and dreams with the suitcase. We were woken up by activity in the corridor: the noise of people coming down, familiar voices calling across to each other. We got up, picked up the suitcase—by now much lighter—grabbed our heaviest coats along with the provisions we had managed to gather, and walked to the door. It was like a reflex. We were blinded by sleep and night and the summoning commotion. We did not even turn back to look at the flat.

Key in hand, you toyed with the options: lock and take the key with us or leave it in the flat and just pull the door? I said, no take it. Sure? you asked. I did not answer. You pulled the door and locked it. You passed the key to me, fittingly handing the passport to our verticality over to me, the traditional guardian of our common stuff, following the usual division of roles: me organised, you absent-minded. But I just then realised I had nowhere to put it. I had space in my pockets, of course, and certainly enough space for a key in my small rucksack. I had mindspace and timespace, I had future holdings and past necessities, I had all that was needed to accommodate the key somewhere in the folds of oblivion. I even had the ultimate argument: come on, it's nothing, it is so light, you never know when you might need it again. But I didn't. I rushed back to the door, opened it with the key, threw the key down somewhere in the hall, and shut the door behind me.

You smiled a timid smile, a tender oscillation between surprise and understanding.

### twenty

We were all there: Luz and Olalekan restless with impatience, Cinder and Toby still carrying stuff down, Selina and her husband all ready and waiting, Marek and Lorna surrounded by heaps of food, various tools, and even cooking accessories. It was the first time we had all gathered in one place and with one common goal. The planks were brimming to the edge with suitcases, bags, food, and water containers. An effervescent readiness was trailing amongst us, our skins, and our belongings.

One would expect noise. Yet we were all quiet— hushed, almost as if we did not want the city to know that we were leaving. Our bodies were lying low, already moving as close as possible to the liquid flatness around us. We were abandoning the verticality that has nourished us all this time, long before the waters, long before us. It felt like a betrayal of the city. We needed to keep this quiet, to soften the blow.

One by one, the vessels of our little fleet were filling with things and people. Toby boarded Selina's skiff, joining the family as if he had always been a part of it. Luz and Olalekan were already floating a little further away from the planks, barely containing their impatience. We were greeted by the old woman, who helped us step onto the boat while carrying our stuff. The boat felt smaller, tidier, more agile than it had last night. We were too excited to sit down, so we stood, slightly helpless and unsure how to contribute, our seafaring inexperience making us overpolite, overly discreet, as if we felt that we needed to be out of the way—a burden of sorts, a cargo that needed to be handled. But she smiled at us, motioning us to one side and getting on with the preparations. Next to us, Marek was readying their little launch, which was predictably piled up with masses of fresh food, tins, and packs of dried food wrapped in valuable plastic. Lorna was still standing on the planks, handing him the last boxes. He stopped abruptly, almost dropping the carton box he was holding, and looked at her. It was too intense, too out of place—something was wrong. Lorna shook her head slowly, not at Marek or at anyone in particular, turned into herself, a sadness melting out of her, a slower water mixing with our agitated surfaces. Don't be silly, Marek said. Lorna just stood there, her head now still, her eyes looking around at our gathering. It was her farewell.

It had never occurred to us that someone might stay behind. It did not make sense in terms of the collectivity we had felt during the night: the whole building ready and breathing as one, all of its bodies on standby and turned towards the same horizon. Although our connection to Lorna had never been particularly close, we felt her decision in our bodies, as if a limb was being cut off. Yet none of us tried to make her change her mind, not even Marek. Her determination was spreading around her with a disarming conviction. It was like an ancient wall that was never erected for us, that did not even address us. We just stood there, our departing enthusiasm blotched by her crossed arms and her serene face. We felt sorry for her, but also overwhelmed by a gigantic feeling of respect for her and her decision. Marek insisted that she keep the launch, or at least some of the food. He even started removing stuff for her to take back, but Lorna stopped him with a gesture full of graceful resolve. I will be fine, she said, and we all heard her.

She looked stronger than any of us, beaming and erect, already looking forward to her solitude. We were worried for her, worried that this show of strength might just be a facade, worried that loneliness would get the better of her. But, in reality, we felt that hers was the better decision. In comparison, our huddling together in enthusiastic anticipation felt too vulnerable, mad even—this following an old woman who was standing there waiting for us, her patience a brittle facade, her actual intention an opaque abyss. We realised we were more concerned about ourselves than about Lorna, sailing away as we were into something that felt like somebody else's dream rather than staying behind in the known safety of the city.

There was something else, too. In retrospect we realised that, had we allowed for the possibility of someone not following, it would indeed have been Lorna. In a way she had always been there, exactly where we wanted to arrive. Her apnoeic diving, her connection to the underwater plants, her increasingly sporadic engagement with the shop and with the rest of us: all these indications of a drifting away towards an aquatic existence much flatter and deeper than our carefully guarded verticality or even our ability to reach the liquid horizontality we seemed to be heading towards.

Looking at her as we were sailing away, still and contained as if she were commanding the waters around her, as if we could not move unless she gently pushed us out, we felt that there were perhaps many ways to reach the same destination. Lorna's way was a solid choice. It was a conscious decision that went against the tide. Ours, on the other hand, felt as inevitable and irresistible as a torrent. No decision, just surrendering. No power to do otherwise, just accepting. It was not even a question of following the old woman's stern encouragement. We were not following her. We were just surrendering, all of us, to something emerging from within us.

There was no question: both Lorna and our own strange little fleet, we were ready. Differently so, but ready. Our readiness was quickening out of the distance between us, right there underneath what used to be our common home.

## twenty-one

Dusk had only just started to break when we reached
the edge of our neighbourhood. We never managed
to follow any kind of fleet formation. It was as if four
unconnected vessels just happened to be going in the
same direction. The speed varied, but it was generally determined by the weakest rower. Everyone
was swapping places, participating in the rowing if
only for brief periods at a time. At one point Cinder
jumped over to Marek's so that he could take over the
rowing, since Marek was the only crew. Later on I
did the same. Despite the unhurried pace, we all got
tired much more easily than we would have done on
a typical day trip. There was tension all around, and
even slowness felt demanding. As soon as the sun became visible on the horizon, strange noises reached
us from Luz and Olalekan's boat. Luz had pulled out
her flute and started playing, interspersing the notes
with soft but piercing cries. The effect was oddly mo-
tivational, as if we were moving into a jungle and becoming one with the fauna. We started responding,
initially jokingly but soon picking up a rhythm.

We attracted the attention of the waking city. Windows opened to see what was happening. A couple
of boats moved alongside and asked us, what is
that, where are you all going, has something happened? We had no answer to any of these questions. We had left the questions back in our flats,
in the building that we used to call home. We took
nothing with us. So we could not answer them. We
kept on telling the truth: no idea, we don't know,
we are just leaving. By now the city was used to
departures. Thousands of people had left the city
early on when the waters first rose. Thousands
more left when we realised that the waters were
here to stay. Thousands kept on leaving every day
in search of their destiny. We were no different.
Yet we felt different. Perhaps this was our fuel, this
sense of difference and necessity that was caused

neither by a fear of wetness nor a longing for still dry ground; rather, our desire was for more wetness.

A different kind of regression.

The day became cold and overcast. We kept at it, tiredness settling like a pain that we needed to breathe through in order to get used to it. At some point when we were reaching the east suburbs, the old woman said, time to stop. She was rowing at the time, but it was clear that she was not tired. She could easily have carried on. Something else made her say it, and loud enough that all of us heard her and turned to look at her. She did something with her oars we had not seen before: she pulled them up and held them erect, like flagless poles pointing to the sky. She held them long enough for the others to follow. She then pulled them in and turned the boat left into a narrow, shaded canal between two relatively low buildings. One by one, all three boats followed us, entering a sort of inevitable formation for the first time.

### twenty-two

We had no means of knowing how the others felt, but the discontent spread like quickfire. For the first time since we had set off, our wondering where we were going hit the surface. It is odd that this happened at that point: this was, after all, just a break, a perfectly normal diversion from the main artery of the city and into a narrower spot that would at any time have afforded us respite from whatever traffic there might have been. Yet this pause—just as perhaps any pause would—threw the blindness of our escape into relief.

So, what's the plan? Selina asked no one in particular. No one answered. We were all looking around us, taking in the area. The old woman had led us to what must have been an old square, large enough for all four vessels to come together around a still visible statue in the middle of the pool. We lassoed our ropes around the mossy horsehead and the brass- feathered hat of its mounting general—or whatever he was—

and gathered around it, our sides bobbing against each other. The square buildings looked derelict, much worse for wear than the rest of the city, with gaping holes in their facades and collapsed roofs that seemed to have taken most of the floors with them. A sound was coming from these buildings, a music of winds and lapping water, nothing we had heard before. The whole square resonated with an atonal ensemble of abandonment, with giant flutes whose holes were always yawning producing all the notes they were capable of simultaneously. Luz started laughing and tried to join in with her flute, making the whole thing even more hysterical and somehow drunken. There was so much tension and so many emotions that we all started screaming and dancing, or at least jumping about in some primordial imitation while trying not to fall over.

Throughout this, we were glancing sideways at the old woman. She kept her distance from the frenzy but did not seem disapproving. It was during that dance, perhaps because of this sympathetic detachment of hers, that it was confirmed in our minds: she was leading us. We were like kids playing under the gaze of the mother. Where this trust came from, nobody could tell. Once we calmed down, she started talking. We will sail for about ten days, perhaps longer. We will stop once during this time and make use of a dry space where we will find water to replenish our supplies. We will need to row without interruption, even at night. We will all be roped up together with a bright orange rope. She would lead the cortege because she was the only one who knew where the shallows lay, with several low-lying buildings and other structures now turned into underwater traps.

We wanted to ask, where are we heading to? We wanted to ask, how do you know all this? We wanted to understand, why are you with us? We asked nothing. We kept looking at one another, slightly breathless from the dance, waiting for someone else to say something, to ask what we all had in mind, but nobody did. Another realisation: our trust in her had to be blind. It would be a constant battle, but it felt right. She emitted an amniotic liquidity; she was calm and enclosed, reassuring in her boundaries. We were all invited into a womb, linked to it by an orange cord. It was almost a relief. The need to be in control was ebbing away from us.

Breathing would become easier. We were sharing fate.

### twenty-three

But the first few days proved much harder than we expected. Those of us more used to rowing were doing most of the work but we quickly reached unspeakable levels of accumulated exhaustion. Night rowing was slower. Easier on the body but more stressful on the whole, because we all had to look out for shallows in the dark.

Our four boats would often reach brief plateaus of synchronised rowing, a breathing continuum that made our arms move to the same rhythm. But it got much harder when fatigue settled in, and we became only marginally more energetic when the old woman stood up and tried to verbalise the rhythm, or when Luz's flute provided some background motivation.

Little by little, without our even realising, our communication with each other was becoming limited to navigational instructions. We only talked to each other during those occasions when we stopped mid water and gathered around to exchange food or other objects—there seemed to be only one pair of scissors, for example, and they somehow became the object that changed hands most frequently. But even these moments were subdued. None of us seemed to have the energy to reach across. We were all part of a slow-moving, whispering hagiography, each vessel occupying its own little space on that liquid altar, all of us separate spheres turned towards the horizon, united only by the presiding mother of some god, her long grey hair the only thing crossing into our individual alcoves.

There was a clear hierarchy that extended to everything. The old woman would eat only after we had eaten. She would row for longer than both of us put together, and also for longer than Toby or Cinder, who would often jump over to our boat to give us a hand. She would become agitated about something, running about and looking over the horizon in an inexplicably frantic way, making us jittery and worried, but she would never share her fears with any of us. She seemed to think that she had sole responsibility for our survival, parcelling out a benevolent distancing and disinvolvement with the same precision as she displayed when navigating the unknown waters. The same strangely awkward situation would occur whenever someone from the other boats tried to attract her attention.

Nobody knew her name. Every time, the same manic gestures and shouts of, excuse me, sorry, hey, to the point that the whole charade became slightly comical. On one occasion, Cinder wanted to jump over to the other boat. He needed to catch her attention in order to make sure the boats converged, but he had to make such an effort that he nearly fell overboard. I could not stop laughing at the slightly irrational situation, and, while touching the woman on her shoulder and pointing to the wildly gesticulating Cinder at the rear boat, I asked her, what's your name anyway? She did not respond, and simply motioned to the others to converge. Come on, this is silly, I insisted. By that time, everyone could hear us. She turned to me and, emitting a fragility that none of us would ever expect from her, she said,

I have forgotten, please don't make me remember.

This disarming show of vulnerability—an indication of a past that was best left undisturbed—was the end of our efforts to learn anything about her. She, on the other hand, knew all of our names, made a point of memorising them, interpellating us whenever she needed, a puppeteer holding us at the edge of her tongue.

The days were melting into each other, with few things to differentiate them. The rowing was relentless. One day early on, we picked up a half-full plastic petrol container that must have floated away from a boat and that was caught on a protruding structure, its seal miraculously watertight. Marek's engine was still working, so he led us along—him first, with the rest of us tugged behind, animated for a few brief hours by a sense of elation, with a breeze against our faces and the horizon brought nearer. But the engine soon spluttered and stopped. Occasionally we would take advantage of a current, and then the only thing we needed to do was steer. But the currents were unreliable and soon had to be abandoned, because they took us in the wrong direction. We also experimented with some makeshift sails. They helped once or twice, but the winds were too weak for them to make a real difference. We did not complain about that, though. We had yet to encounter a storm in that suburban ocean, and we were only too glad not to.

By now we had left the city behind. We were following the general flow, slowly making our way in some vaguely easterly direction. There was nothing to look at, nothing to distract us from the tiredness, just watery emptiness. We were in the deep, flat countryside, dipped into a monochromatic seamlessness, sky and water melting into each other's grey, clouds punctuating our confused sense of direction. Sometimes we would peer into the water below us, trying to discern some sunken human structure. Out here the waters were a bit clearer. No longer the usual thick green, they were reminiscent of a dirty, agitated sea, with brown and golden flecks reflecting back the light and still deflecting us from their deeper secrets. We did spot the occasional factory lying low on the seabed. We were usually alerted to them by the top part of their chimneys, still sticking out like forgotten promises of human vanity.

On some occasions we crossed other boats, usually small and solitary, but there was no recognition, no call out—just an embarrassed silence, like when we used to see someone we knew but did not feel like acknowledging and we put on airs of busy diffidence in order to avoid meeting their gaze. The strangest encounter, however, must have been on the second night. The sky was overcast and starless, a blanket of darkness covering our movements. We spotted a light on the horizon, and it soon became clear that this was no static structure. In comparison to our slow rowing it was moving towards us at an inconceivable speed. We started waking everyone up to see this exoplanetary vision, all the time asking the old woman and each other what it could be, but no one could guess with any certainty. It soon towered over us: a repurposed cruiser, a colossal presence of darkness with flashes of kerosene light, a peremptory displacement of air, water, and night. It went past so fast that we were left rocking wildly in its wake, wondering whether we had really seen such a thing. How did it move, who was onboard, where was it heading? All questions that increased our sadness and isolation, making the night cold reach deeper into our bodies.

We would often edge past clusters of unidentifiable structures that protruded from the water or lay just below the surface. We learned to identify the latter by the way in which their flatness looked even flatter and more uniform than the rest of the water, like a layer of saliva on wet skin. On windy days we could see the waves change, announcing something ahead of us large enough to disturb the usual flow. Our sense of smell complemented our vision and helped us avoid the largest hurdles: in that liquid desert, the odours of the various protrusions—be they metal, brick, wood, vegetal or animal matter—reached our sensitive noses in time for the necessary manoeuvring.

The old woman had a particular way of signalling these hurdles, something between a whistle and a groan, her arm lifted in the direction of the shallows.

She seemed to have an innate knowledge of the waters. It was easy to rely on her and to forget how treacherous the waters really were. Luz started joining us at the front and increasingly worked together with the old woman to make sure we steered clear of traps. Hesitantly, the old woman started taking longer naps, trusting us to spot problems and preserving her energy for the nights, when things were much more hazardous.

At some point, perhaps on the fourth day, our fleet sailed past the outskirts of another large city. We tried to guess which one it was. Several names came up, but no one could recognise with certainty any landmark in the horizon. It was a strange moment for our caravan, looking from afar at a city's central district, with its taller buildings jutting out from the surface and the whole submerged infrastructure of the periphery poking up here and there, creating a sort of grey noise. We should have been feeling nostalgic or at least curious to go in and see what had happened to the city, to meet other people, maybe, or just to look for provisions. We did nothing. Even if it had been up to us—which it wasn't, since the old woman seemed to be totally oblivious of the city—we still would not have done anything like that. If anything, we felt that in this way we were sealing our departure.

### twenty-four

Our first, and as it turned out only, act of rebellion took place quite early on, during our first evening in the sea, when we were still in the eastern suburbs of the city. In a barely controlled voice cracking with tiredness, Luz said aloud something that had been lurking beneath the surface of our consciousness: but why must we row at night too? What's the rush?

She shouted it across the four vessels, obviously addressing the old woman, but in the process summoning support from all of us. Although adrenaline was still running high and the idea of keeping at it was not yet tempered by what was soon to become extreme fatigue, we nodded in agreement. Because, more than the fear of night rowing, more than the need to rest, there was another, implicit question in Luz's protest: is this not just an escape? is there somewhere specific we are trying to reach?

The old woman stopped what she was doing and looked at Luz.

We are already late, she said.

It is already April, days are getting hotter. Yes, so? Luz carried on. We can still row during the day, it's not too hot yet. It's not about that, the old woman said. We have limited provisions. We have loads of food, several of us protested, half-aloud, half-mumbling. Who's going to eat all that? The old woman went back to tying a complicated knot and, without looking at anyone in particular, simply said, it's about arriving on time. We are already late.

But arriving where? And what are we late for? Nobody dared to ask. Luz shrugged and looked around at the rest of us. We could not intervene. We did not want to ask anything more. We were too afraid of an answer that might have tied us down. Our readiness, our dawn-break escape, and our irreversible departure had left us unmoored to swim with an almost primeval sense of freedom. Our route was a line of flight, not a line towards a destination. We really wanted to believe this. It opened up the planet's gentle curvature for us to explore. And, deep down, we were also desperate to avoid disappointment.

### twenty-five

It must have been the morning of the fifth day. On our boat, the old woman had been rowing since dawn. We were fast asleep on the deck, curved into each other with whatever blankets we could muster piled on top of us. The sudden lack of movement jerked us out of sleep. I sat up and saw the woman holding the oars up, as she had done the first time we all stopped at that little square in our city. The others gathered around, mid-ocean, on that smooth limpid day, the rowers stretching and massaging their arms, the sleepers slowly awakening.

We are about to reach our resting point, she said. We will stop there for the day. Before that, however, we need to cross a river. Although it is underwater and at one with the rest of the waters, the current is very strong and makes the whole area rush and froth. We will cross on the site of an old train bridge. We will use some of the oars to push against the bridge, and the rest to keep on rowing. Cinder, move over to Marek's, we need two on each boat. If one of us is taken by the current, we all perish. There are rapids further downstream. We have no choice; we must cross here.

What is a river? What is a body of water on a planet filled with water? We could not understand. Her reply was, it is still a river. But how can it be? We soon saw it with our own eyes. In the middle of the flatness that we had got so used to in the past few days, planted almost arbitrarily and somehow capriciously, naked and unfathomable, devoid of riverbeds, riparian communities or weeping willows, surrounded by endless liquid as thick as itself, there it was: a direction, a movement without boundaries, a rush so assimilated by its surroundings that it felt as if there was nothing outside it, as if the whole planet was moving along in that one irreversible direction. The river that lay beneath the leagues of waters had expanded to become an uncontrollable current, invisible and insidiously mighty. The roar was unbearable, a frothy fury striking against what was left of an arched bridge that had already been flooded by the rush of the flatness.

We all started rowing harder. The old woman was yelling, one-*two* one-*two*, her voice all of a sudden a force of nature, a roar booming above the roar: *one* round and smoothing the ground for the gigantic *two*; *one* a preparation, *two* a plunge into oceanic depths; *one* quieter but still booming, *two* a stentorian scream of salvation. One-*two* one-*two*, two numbers that would make the difference between crossing and being swept away; they were lashed on our arms and backs, forcing everyone to obey like automata, controlling everything, from our arms to our breath. We reached the beginning of the bridge. The old woman stood up, practically throwing one oar to you while grabbing the other, and, without missing a beat, pushed hers against the first pillar of the bridge. This was our first lever. The fleet moved more slowly now, each boat planting its oar on the bridge to hold us in place. There was shouting and panic, with half of us standing up, unwilling gondoliers on a sinking planet, oars extended from our trembling arms as we tried to keep our balance against the bridge, while the others continued to row, drenched on the decks and almost swallowed by the rapids.

I was behind you, supporting you in the rowing, sliding on the wet deck, constantly falling off balance and ending up crashing at the other end of the boat. We were heading the fleet because of the old woman who commanded our and everybody else's movements—but there was no real head. Our boat was one little part of a gigantic Chinese dragon dancing through the streets of a drowned city, all fragmented yet all part of one unbroken line. We were united by a rush that matched the rapids. Our bodies were raging, ablaze with fire amidst the deluge. We were emanating a scorching redness, each fragment of the dragon a moment of our collective breath, the blaring numbers like the rhythm of triumphant drums, the burning oxygen of our exhalations and the evaporating heat of our sweat our shields against the frenzy of the flood.

This was the first time that we were exposed to such fury. Up until then the waters had been rising slowly, subterraneously, a relentlessly gentle act of unhurried destruction. But this was different: we were encountering a force we had almost forgotten.

All of a sudden, our apartment, our city, our entire lives preceding that moment felt like places of sepulchral oblivion, traps of stagnation, a snowball that no one would ever shake. Faced with the titanic force of the water, drunk on the adrenaline of a different death or a different life, we were rowing.

In the midst of all this, I felt something that was so out of place that I tried to censor it immediately. I would have managed to forget all about it—it was not that hard after all in that maelstrom—if it hadn't been for the spray of a wave hitting me across the face with so much force that it was as if someone had actually slapped me. I woke up to the most incongruous sensation—or perhaps an actual realisation: it was as if, miraculously, reluctantly, roaringly, the water was joining in our strife, becoming part of our battle, not the enemy but the connecting ally, a quashing benevolence, a violent acceptance, melting our fragments together, giving wings to our dragon. It was the water and not the bridge that was helping us. The bridge was old verticality, a ruin of a rotting nostalgia. It was nothing in comparison to the water.

The water was delivering us.

We were one with it, becoming part of the ancient river, helping it bloat and distend to cover the whole future.

I took your place in the rowing seat, propelling even more eagerly than before, feeling connected with everyone else in a mad elation. We reached the end of the bridge but had to keep on rowing with the same force, cutting across the river—this vast new river that took in its rush the whole known world, kilometres of fury that fanned out to an imperceptible gradation before finally reaching the calm and gentleness of the other side.

We made it. We might have reached the edge of the river some time before, or perhaps just then—we could not tell. The waters had moved.

From now on, calmness would always be pregnant with fury.

## twenty-six

A building was beckoning from the depths of the flatness. Incongruously tall, defiantly isolated, it emerged on our horizon shortly after the river crossing. From a distance it looked like a lighthouse, becoming thinner and lighter as it rose, ending up almost translucent at the top. It must have been at least thirty floors high. We recognised it immediately, although we had no idea that we had already reached that far— it was built by one of those global celebrity architects a decade ago and inaugurated to much fanfare. It was the tallest structure in an otherwise low-lying but exquisitely manicured area, with such state-of-the-art facilities as the uber-rich could be convinced to invest in for their absurdly expensive apartments, complete with helipads and ultrafast infrastructure that gave direct access to the river marina.

The only thing left standing now was the upper part of the main building, seductively capturing the sun, a lighthouse of an invitation.

We managed to glide on a current that made our rowing a bit easier. But it was still a good few hours' hard work before we finally came under the building's long shadow as it cut across the water. Up close our impressions changed. The building had been ravaged by the elements, its defiant prominence becoming its downfall. It was as if endless monsoons had been falling upon it without respite. Its facade was entirely covered in a sort of climbing moss that had turned brown and slimy at the same time, choking the building's every aperture and protrusion, every panoramic window and helipad. The astonishing thing was that it was still standing. Not only that, but it was clearly thriving.

We could hear sounds we had not heard in a long time, noises of industry and toil, sounds of music and leisure, calls of sociality and connection. We smelled long-forgotten odours of food, mountain herbs, and even whiffs of rich perfume. This was a city away from the city. We felt apprehensive, but the old woman seemed confident. She led us toward the back of the building, where a whole infrastructure of docks, floating garden boxes filled with growing vegetable plants, giant machines that were producing some sort of energy, and an elaborate network of ladders and platforms were both inviting and intimidating. We docked and were checked by some people at what looked like the central gates of the tower. Fatigue, dizziness, and unpreparedness for all this made us ungrateful guests, mumbling and looking around like helpless children. The old woman seemed to know some people, although her behaviour remained evasive. She clearly knew her way around, though, and she led us up to dry ground on a higher floor. The floor was split into compartments that housed scattered mattresses and other paraphernalia, weathered and stationary as if they had been lying around in the punishing humidity for far too long.

This is their inn, she said. It is a short stopover. We pay them in kind and they help us with refuge for the night and water. We will give them some of the food we brought along. If any of you want to stay here rather than carry on, let me know and I can put you in touch with the right people. Otherwise, just rest. We are leaving tomorrow morning.

It was as if the last remaining drops of energy had been sucked off us, our bodies melting on the spot. This was the most terrifying thing we had had to do since setting off. The freedom to choose, served to us in such a normalising and non judgemental way, was paralysing. We huddled together and tried to understand where we stood with it all. We had not seen anything of the upper floors, we knew nothing about this place, yet we were certain that this was as close to a social organisation as we could possibly hope to encounter. Overhead, sounds of people moving stuff, walking or running, talking or calling each other, were pulling us up like drawstrings, our necks craned towards the invisible familiarity of belonging. We were battling with fear and desire, uncertainty about either staying or going, nostalgia for human society, and a lassitude towards what this society might mean.

The old woman had left us. We could not ask her either about this place or about where we were heading to. How were we supposed to decide between two unknown coordinates?

More agonising questions started cropping up: could this be a trap? Do we trust her? What if this is some sort of slave trade and we are the payment in kind? Should we just escape while we can? The fears were getting deeper and crazier; walls of insecurity and dread were being erected around us and between us with every new thought. This was supposed to be a restful pause, but it turned out to be the most stressful thing imaginable.

Little by little, Marek started bringing some calm. His reasoning always felt unhurried, natural, and honest. He always tried to mediate, to lower the temperature and ground us in a reality as inescapable as it was hopeful. It was as if he was bringing back, right there in that draughty, dirty floor, the whole garden shop that he had once managed, with its salvaged plants, trees and climbers, herbs and flowers, and placing them once again all around us. We were being enclosed in a lush aquiferous jungle dripping with moisture and breath, our shoulders and backs caressed by the shade of the thick leaves, our lungs opening up to the saturated scent of slowly rotting roots. He brought in death as a possibility and spread it there like a mucous moss touching our feet. And so what, he made us feel. So, it is a possibility. But this is where we start from, this is where we end. He planted a little water lily in the middle of it, its round leaf a platform for gathering around and listening to the world bubbling past. He shaded us with a weeping willow as tall as the whole building, the ends of its cascading branches nestling in our hands like toys.

We saw that there was no choice. And this was our freedom.

We slowly withdrew from one another, our bodies tilting like stems, folding into embraces with those nearest to us or falling into formations that felt right. I looked around and took in our curled-up collective body, a tired dragon nursing its wounds. I reached out to you, your body heat an inviting salon for our thoughts and feelings. I made myself comfortable in your chambers, wrapped myself in the afternoon light of your presence. This was the first time the two of us had truly felt together since we had set off, free from the gaze of the old woman. I heard your promise and I whispered it back to you: we are still here. We have not lost each other in the larger us. We are still connected to the others, but also withdrawn, an amoeba gently shrinking into itself and its self-loving. We are a fractal of that larger body, one with it yet singular and distinct.

I breathed your breath.

We shut our eyes and abandoned ourselves to this ground that was not moving. We knew—or perhaps we just felt it? was it all of us at the same time, or just us? or someone perhaps commented on it just before slumber took us all? or perhaps nothing happened, just a whisper of a knowledge, but with a promise as loud as the sky—I don't know, but we knew that this might be the last time we surrendered ourselves to a ground that was not moving.

### twenty-seven

We were woken up by the old woman. Unexpectedly gentle, crouching next to each one of us, carefully touching our shoulders and whispering that old affirmation, a code whose signification eluded everyone,

are you ready

and we all knew what we had to do. One by one our bodies stretched into a long, soft awakening, spectacularly clashing with the drab conditions of the inn around us. A wave of gratitude was pushing us up; we were happy finally to have rested, happy to have survived the night, happy to be leaving.

The sounds of the slowly waking tower accompanied us across a long distance in the water. The day was opening around us, and even the old woman was smiling. I asked her, did you think anyone would stay behind? She looked at me solemnly, as if she knew I would understand, and said, I would have been disappointed if anyone had chosen to stay behind. I trusted you right from the start. Trusted us to do what? I asked. And she said, this. What you are doing. She shook her head reassuringly, reading the doubt on my face. It's alright. You are doing the right thing.

The next days were slow but somehow felt propelled by a different energy. We were more than halfway there, we would finally encounter whatever our fate was, we were closer to that horizon. Our rowing was smoother, our jumping from boat to boat light and playful, even our discussions across the boats were more animated.

We were arriving.

## twenty-eight

On the morning of that final day, our convoy faced some unusually strong currents. It was important that we rowed against them, the old woman urged. She was encouraging us, keeping us to the rhythm, but the mood was different, jubilant and teasing. The rowing was almost as hard as when we crossed the bridge but, she said, be grateful for these currents, they are your walls and moat. They will keep everyone away but the most determined.

The currents subsided as abruptly as they had started. We glided over an invisible bump on the surface of the water, and, just like that, the angry froth was replaced by smoothness. We rowed for a couple of hours in the late morning sun.

At one point, quite unannounced by our surroundings, the old woman lifted her arm and signalled us to row slower. As far as we could tell, the landscape had not changed. The same flat endlessness, the same reflecting surface, the same cupola of a sky holding us in. But she seemed to see something different, to know that we had arrived somewhere, to be looking for something in particular. We too became attentive to our surroundings, listening out for different sounds, rowing in a reconnoitring, quiet way, ready to be surprised. I was at the back of the fleet with Marek, helping with the rowing and feeling a locked-up tension battling against invisible walls. I was excited, we all were, but also fearful—what if we are disappointed? What if there is nothing after all?

And then she lifted her oars up, pointing to the sky. We were right in the middle of everything, with nothing to mark a difference, nothing to hook onto. We were folded in a grey sameness. We didn't understand.

She turned to the rest of us and announced, we have arrived.

Where?

There was nothing. I wanted to cry. Selina was having a hysterical reaction, are you joking? what is this? most of us were numb and helpless, just looking around in despair. I started thinking about going back  do we have enough water, how about food, perhaps we would be welcomed to the tower—all the while feeling the need to come over and be held by you. You were looking across the boats, beyond the water and the air, straight into me, summoning a response from me, perhaps hoping for support or reassurance, but I had nothing.

And then the old woman said, just walk out, it's safe. Nobody understood her at first until Toby, bravado mixed with annoyance, jumped out. His landing was unexpected, vertiginously shallow, childlike. He nearly fell over. But he managed to stand up. The water was coming up to his thighs. He turned to us and laughed, it is warm! One by one, we started sliding in.

The temperature and smoothness of the water made us feel as if we were taking an antediluvian bath, a long-forgotten luxury. Our skin was co-extensive with the boundless pool around us. We squatted and allowed the water to cover our upper bodies, giggling like toddlers in a bathtub, wavelets plopping against our chins. For that brief moment, our initial despair was put aside. We were all in that shallow pool, even the old woman who seemed for the first time to forget all about us and do something just for herself. She turned her back on us and, covered by the shallow water, was lightly bobbing up and down. Nobody felt like getting up. We were all floating in that new yet ever so old sense of belonging, joyfully glistening like warm vegetables coated in fresh green olive oil. The light was slanting on our faces like a caress from above. Even the scents were different to the usual ones. There was a vegetable smell surging as if from below, like softly rotting leaves, and even a light waft of fresh herbs, rosemary rolling down a slope and thyme drying under a hot summer sun. Was that just our imagination? Were we galloping towards a return to a past that was no longer?

The first to come out of the water was Selina. She propped herself up and, in yet another gesture from the past, climbed elegantly up onto the side of the boat, tied her hair up, and looked around for a towel with which to dry. Little by little we all started coming out, except for the old woman, who stayed in, oblivious to us. We gathered in Marek's launch, lying around or sitting with our knees huddled against our chests, a semblance of a beach party after a good swim.

We were waiting.

She eventually joined us. But something had changed. She sat amongst us rather than, as usual, standing up giving us instructions. Her face was softened, the lines of hardship accumulated over the last few days almost erased. She even assumed the same relaxed yet expectant posture as the rest of us. She was now one of us, or perhaps we had finally become worthy of her. A sense of achievement spread amongst us. We were a little smug, a little drunk with the pleasure of the warm shallow water—unjustifiable in view of the fact that we were still in the middle of nothing.

I will stay with you for as long as you need me, she started. I will show you your new home. This is the closest there is to Eden. We looked at her askance. She continued, there is warm and cold drinking water from underground sources pouring into these shallow waters. There are acres of seaweed you can harvest. There are water corridors so full of fish that they push against each other and jump out of the surface, ready to land in your hands. There is strong weathered wood lying around that we will use to build what we need. And we are now anchored right at our most valuable asset: the ricefields.

Is there rice here? asked Olalekan. There will be, she said. This is why we needed to be here on time. It is already the end of June, almost too late to plant, but I think we can manage. We will deal with this first thing in the morning.

### twenty-nine

Our first night at what we would call ricefields, and would eventually be calling home, was unlike any other night we had experienced.

As usual, we started by making sleeping areas in our boats, tired from the day's rowing, a mixture of disappointment and questioning hope in our minds. Mid way through this, you stopped and leaned out of the boat, your arm extended, touching the water. Your fingers lightly broke the surface, burnished ebony speckled by a lattice of stars promising warmth and oblivion. You looked at me and smiled. This was your invitation to play, and I had learned to recognise that childlike smile that could have meant so many things, though, in this context—and this context was never something I could describe in detail, because I did not know what it was that made it special, perhaps it was not the context of our surroundings so much as the context of the connection between you and me, or that reverberation of your desire in me, or perhaps our mutual reverberation of a grander desire, at the same time in us and larger than us, I don't know—I always knew what that smile meant.

Let's play.

And there you were, sliding in the water again, an effortless move as if the boat no longer had any sides and the water had flooded its interior, ushering you out like a spoon carrying a precious bite into the mouth of a lover, and so you glided in the glimmering surface, soft dark green blankets sucking you in, and I followed you.

This time, it felt like a return. We embraced, aroused by each other's bodies, looking at each other as if for the first time since we had started the journey, rowing fit and glistening naked, smoothed over in the evening water. I wanted you and you wanted me, yet there was something else there too: animals and plants and elements were part of our desire, howling beasts that carried us on their backs, their sprouting arches thrusting us up into the night sky, sinuous seaweed wrapping itself around our limbs and bondaging us to the world, indigo swordfish inserting themselves into our open oceans, gold-speckled mud sucking us in and burying us in a suffocating ecstasy, and, of course, above all, water, slow warm water moulded between our bodies and folded around us like a lagoon waiting for the tide.

And there were other humans too, a small amphitheatre of spectators, four boats circled around our waterbed, eight other sleeping areas left half-done, eight bodies eventually sliding in with us, joining us in a celestial constellation lightly trembling on the surface of our new waters. Were we sky or planet, where is the line separating the city from the wolves?

We were becoming our horizon.

Ten necks, twenty shoulders, twenty more arms tensing to hold up a different sky. Sex in that cosmic womb among our four boats was not just a matter of curiosity. Yes, we were curious, and yes, we were exploring a tension that had perhaps been piling up during the journey—even celebrating our arrival by entering this reality naked and available. But it was more than just carnal desire; we were more than just human flesh. We were partaking of the flesh of the world, feasting on each other's bodies, forgetting whatever genders, sexualities, species we felt we had been assigned so far. We became jellyfish, tentacles, transparency. Our collective skin, bathed in this new, slower darkness, became ten little spots lighting up and spreading across the ricefields, luminous presences of stars gone by. We were looking down at ourselves: a constellation whose name had not yet been uttered, landed on the other side of the universe.

The earth has been thrown off balance. It has plunged into a shallow pool of oblivion, decentred for good. The old throne is rotting in a sea of human urine. The sceptre running from pole to pole is decapitated. Orb is no more. All that is left is these little scattered lights, a few among many, no brighter than any others but linked up in a network of gently glistening fungi trails. We were infinitesimal side-nothings, afterthoughts, antibodies.

Our breathing was mediated by the dying planet.

We were all breathing with it, foretasting its end, reverberating with each other's breath, one body with multiple chthonic genitalia, joy and rage colliding through our splashing bodies.

How to become both everything and nothing, everywhere and yet totally absent, full of voice yet void—all this we learned that night and in the nights after that first night. We entered a wheel of repetition in that cosmic womb. Distances were negotiated anew every time, and intimacy was mediated by our desire for the world. Our nights became subterranean, collective, and wet.

We never returned to our sleeping areas. We learned to fall asleep while floating on water, our

faces illuminated by the glowing night sky, our eyes
never entirely closed, our bodies one with the flatness around us, merging our will with that of the
flow and gently bumping into each other; I am here,
said my thigh to your foot, I am still here, whispered
your ear to his shoulder, I will stay here, promised
her arm to my knee.

And so what if no one will ever know the name
of this new constellation of desires that we have set
up in the space between earth and sky? We are already part of the grand oblivion. We were born in
the epoch of Lethe, when the earth started forgetting its most aggressive inhabitant, cleansing itself
of us with a ceremonial bath that would last a few
decades. We were already molecules of the future,
machines that wallow in their own self-annihilation.
We were granted this last breath, gurgling and asth-
matic, filled with moisture and flatness. We are now
exhaling it, holding hands.

### thirty

Give me your water boxes, she said, as soon as we
woke up.

We climbed back onto our boats, familiar spaces
turned strange, and rummaged through our stuff.
After the previous night's experience these boxes
appeared trivial. We felt invincible. We felt we had
opened a new door, in this world where doors were
no longer relevant. We nearly fell into that all-too-
human trap of heroics and triumphalism, heady
with our newly forged fleshy tribe. Who had time for
gadgets and gimmicks now that we had truly discovered each other? But the old woman would not
let go. She had returned to her usual rough self, ef-
ficient and curt. We handed her the boxes, our skins
wrinkled by the night plunge, our almost translucent
fingers barely shading the rectangular plastic boxes. The murky substance inside them was stirring
slowly, crudely. She made us move the boats a bit

further along—but why we could not tell. The same flatness everywhere. Everything seemed to us to be just the same. But we had learned to trust her. She stood on the side of the boat, arms held out over the water. She held the first box up, twisted her fingers this way and that, and after a while the box opened up, releasing its murky liquid into the water. She did the same with all of the boxes, one after the other, moving from one boat to the other, allowing the liquid to land in adjacent spots in the water. And now we wait, she says.

Wait for what? Olalekan asks. We were never given a box, what is that all about? Luz shakes her head vehemently next to him, looking at us in an accusatory way, feeling excluded. We wait for the rice to grow, says the old woman. These boxes contain deepwater rice seeds. The liquid preserved them while preventing them from sprouting. They are airtight. They are your future. I will show you how to take care of the sprouts, how to shelter them from bad weather, how to sow. Why did we not get one, asks Luz? You just didn't, says the old woman. You were not there when that stranger visited us, I volunteer. And by the way, who was he? I ask, knowing I will get no reply but hoping to divert the discussion to something other than the box. A fear grips me. This never-given box might become the apple in the garden: knowledge denied, the snake awoken.

We are looking at each other, ready to dismiss the whole thing as inconsequential, the taste of flesh on our lips being far too potent for this kind of division. But a seed has been planted.

It does not mean anything, the old woman says. If the others are willing to share their crop with you, it does not mean anything.

### thirty-one

A few weeks later, the seeds started sprouting. It would not be long now before our first harvest.

Meanwhile, the old woman had shown us how to live among the truly plentiful offerings of our new home. She helped us to construct small floating huts for when the weather was turning, to devise ways of getting easy access to drinking water, to choose the right seaweed to harvest, to dry and use seaplants that had medicinal qualities (their smell reminding us of lemon thyme and coriander), to distinguish the edible jellyfish species, and to store fish for days during periods when they might be less bountiful than usual. She was showing us ways of dealing with potential futures, but her focus was always the present. In some ways, ours was too. We had lived long enough in the future, fearing collapse, illness, lack of provisions. That we had been offered the opportunity to be folded into an eternal present was something we still could not fully believe. The area was so well protected by the currents and the surrounding rapids that it was as if it was suspended in perennial calmness. The water rarely became more than a gently waving surface, and even when the rain was falling—sometimes for days on end and, increasingly, more frequently—we could take refuge in the huts or just splay ourselves in the water, exposing ourselves to the lack of difference between up there and down here.

The old woman left us quite abruptly one morning, when the weather had turned unusually warm. We knew she was going to leave some day, but thought that it would happen after the first rice crop. We suspected nothing, even when she started explaining the process to us, the first actions to take as soon as the sprouts reached metre-high, the storage issues, the preservation of seeds for the next crop—or even when she brought out a water box that she had apparently never opened and had kept safe in case this crop failed, and showed us how to break it open if we ever needed to. We were sure that she would stay with us, if not for ever then at least for a long period that could not be easily punctuated by a departure. She had become part of our collective bodies, diurnal and nocturnal.

Her skin was a fragment of our skin, her flesh another tentacle of our new being. How could she leave?

### thirty-two

A few days before she left us, she and I were having a quiet conversation about how best to maintain the boats so that they did not rot. She was astonishingly knowledgeable, and always imparted both the techniques she had mastered over the years and her resourceful intelligence without a hint of hesitation. Her open, self-effacing willingness to help reminded me of that stranger who had left behind the water box that had brought us here. There was something about the melancholic way in which he had sat down with us for dinner, something about the readiness and forbearance with which he fixed our broken window. He had hardly lain down during the night, and he had left the following morning without a word. All that was strangely consonant with the old woman's behaviour. Who was this man? I asked again, under my breath, not addressing her or anyone in particular, just wondering, a resigned whisper in the face of an event that was destined to remain forever unexplained. And in the same way, under her breath and scattered in the direction of the water, the syllables melting into each other, she murmured,

I am that man.

We no longer bring ourselves to believe in gods or divine presences. The categories belonging to such a way of thinking were gone for ever. We were left only with bodies and their movement in space and time.

Nothing else could fit in.

The divine was something we could not accommodate, that we would not accommodate. And so we left this revelation there, floating among us, still a part of us, neither divine nor immaterial, unable to elevate us to a higher plane of existence, too proximate to become an aspiration for us.

We became neither more nor less divine after this, neither more nor less human.

We just remained floating.

So, when she left, she took with her that breath, and our skins grew back to cover the patch of her absence.

### thirty-three

In all this, you and I were trying to find ourselves. Our love for each other grew wider and deeper. You were always you and I was always me, but we multiplied. There were now all the others too. One evening, after a few nights of shared flesh and waters, when our collective body was becoming ever stronger and more confident of itself, we felt we needed each other more than usual. But just each other. The sun had not set yet. We still had some time. We started raising a little bit of water around us, a wavelet at a time, as if we were burying ourselves in sand, but this time, like expert brick layers spreading sheets of transparency, we were placing one thick slice of water on top of the other, erecting around us a small igloo made of prisms. When the wall was high enough, we folded ourselves into its cavity, hiding our bodies behind it but showing all the others that our contours were still there, that what isolated us was the same thing that was holding us all together. The setting sun was pouring through the water strata, drenching our little wall with a fire burning as if from within. I cannot remember what we did in there, how we spent our aquatic intimacy, whether we were happy afterwards or just blushing with embarrassment, whether we were reminded of our little boudoir in the city or whether we felt adrift in the flatness despite the wall. Whatever happened, that was the last time you and I did anything like that. Just like everything else, our melancholia at having lost each other was washed away by the plenitude of our extensions.

We had become a school of bodies.

Our skin was becoming permeable, and, along with the water, a different otherness was seeping in. Our ability to differentiate between human, fish, plant, or element was becoming flattened. Our ability to love was growing, spreading its force to the elements but losing its human focus. We were becoming the world, co-extensive with everything else within it.

### thirty-four

We knew that things would change. We knew that children would be born among us, and that our amphibian awkwardness would be slowly perfected over the next generations. We also knew that the planet was changing beyond recognition and that the horizontality we had chosen was going to become the unavoidable destiny of all survivors.

There was a tacit agreement among us not to wilfully witness the world's traumatic passage. The ricefields seemed to have immersed us in a state of contentment, and we were afraid we might shatter it if we were to come into contact with anyone from the outside. We never talked about the tower we had seen on our journey, and no passing cruise-ship ever haunted our nights with its phantom lights. After an initial period when our nights were ravaged by drowning nightmares, our dreams slowly turned into lulling excursions along sleep's deep seabed, their meaning as fluid and indecipherable as the ricefields around us.

But we also knew that, no matter where we slept, with whom we slept, or what we dreamed, some things would not change. We knew that we remained human animals despite our slowly adapting skins and our aquatic dreams. The seeds of division had been planted, mixed in with the rice seeds. Without ever having talked about it, we knew that we all feared the harvest. We had not yet divided anything up except tasks. We seemed to have left all concepts of property behind, virginal bodies in a virginal world where lines had never been drawn. But we knew that we carried these lines in our bodies, engraved on our bellies and thighs—scars of a civilisation that demanded our submission, traces of an animality that demanded our preponderance.

Nothing has cropped up yet, and the ricefields are so only in name. We keep on frolicking, choosing to forget that we are waiting for something that might break us.

We are all willingly stranded in the shallows of the lake covering the globe, neither human nor beast, steeped in the tepid and uncreased water that barely rises to our knees, each one of us drowning in the melancholy of the desire for something other than what we have.

# waterspeak

Shush.

Sleep now.

Because then, you sometimes dream. That's when you come closer to me. Your dreams last seconds and span centuries. You understand me then. You become me then.

This bunch is trying to turn its life into a dream. They are dreaming of never waking up. They become their own lullaby. They trail the edge of their breath over to where the night sleeps.

And they become the water's dream: the other water.

I am still listening.

Sometimes from within, a mesh in a mesh, and sometimes from a distance—and even then, I am rarely far away. Just at the end of an oar or on the lip of an ocean.

I have never stopped listening.

But, for a while now, I've only been hearing one voice. It is as if the previous voices, the two lovers and their touches, the crisp skin of their togetherness, the supple vowels of their evenings, it's as if all that has become quietly ensconced in this new voice. It is still a soft voice but vibrating with a raspiness, an echo of sorts. Legatos of difference, stutters of otherness, and staccatos of assimilation lie next to one another in this voice.

It feels like a slice of other water, sliding into my entrails.

Its temperature is slightly high and its texture silk-soft, an iridescent snail signature lodging itself across my meteors. It is a friendly visit.

I will play with it for a while.

It has come as far as it can. It can go no further. I, of course, know this. I see it like I see a crystal: perfect refraction, the same image on every cut, always the same fractal repetition.

They will never change.

They doze off into lulls, they allow themselves to evaporate while they float immobile under the sun, they forget their limbs when they all become one sinuous desire. They want to forget, they are trying so hard under their amphibian skin, they spread and spill, they flow and fly, they do everything right. They think they have a chance.

They dream that the water is other.

But it is not. I know it.

And they know it too, because they, too, are water.

How to make this easier for them? I guess the same goes even for me—how to make it easier for me, their listener and echoing chamber, their enabler and destroyer.

Well, I cannot.

I cannot make it easier. I can only make the wound ooze more rushingly and our liquids become thicker, as the planet turns towards its last dusk.

Through this wound, we might all, one day, eventually flow together across our distance.

## acknowledgments

This book is indebted to my sister Christina for knowing how to read water; Riccardo Baldissone, Fran Bigman, Victoria Brooks for focussing always on the lovers; Alex Buxton for his generous and sensitive reading; Roswitha Gerlitz for the Brazil beginnings; Jason Katz for inhabiting the spaces of the book; Sakis Kyratzis for finding it hard-going; Michelle Lovric for sharing her insights during those long writing days and deep water days; Demetra Papidaki for her patience and ideas.

Heartfelt thanks go to Lunds Universitet and the Pufendorf Institute of Advanced Studies for the Fellowship on Urban Creativity that set the wheels in motions; ERIS: Alex Stavrakas for the confidence in my writing and Angus Ledingham for his precision; Danielle Arnaud for her love and trust and for inviting the 2023 art exhibition *A Constellation of Conduits Was Channelled Between Us, and Our Distance Became Water*–based on this book–along with Robert Cervera for the most careful reading ever done and the soundscape of my aquatic dreams and fears; Elias Avramidis for his always wise comments and our summer of sage waters;

*and Venice for everything else.*

# ERIS

86–90 Paul Street
London EC2A 4NE

265 Riverside Drive
New York NY 10025

Copyright © Andreas Philippopoulos-Mihalopoulos 2024

The right of Andreas Philippopoulos-Mihalopoulos to be identified as
the author of this work has been asserted in accordance with Section 77
of the Copyright, Designs and Patent Act 1988.

ISBN 978-1912475-48-3

eris.press

ANDREAS PHILIPPOPOULOS-MIHALOPOULOS is an academic / artist / fiction author. His practice includes legal theory / performance / ecological pedagogy / lawscaping / performance lecture / video art / spatial justice / moving-poems / critical autopoiesis / online performance / radical ontologies / installation art / picpoetry / performance machines / fiction writing / sculpture / wave-writing / political geography / clay making / gender and queer studies / painting / continental philosophy / posthumanism / anthropocenes. He is Professor of Law & Theory at the University of Westminster, and Director of The Westminster Law & Theory Lab. His academic books include the monographs *Absent Environments* (2007), *Law, Justice, Society* (2009), and *Spatial Justice: Body Lawscape Atmosphere* (2014). His collection of stories *Book of Water* is published in Greek (Thines, 2017) and English (ERIS, 2022). His art practice has been shown at Palais de Tokyo, the 58th Venice Art Biennale 2019, the 16th Venice Architecture Biennale 2016, the Tate Modern, Inhotim Instituto de Arte Contemporânea Brazil, Arebyte Gallery, Ca' Pisani Venice, Danielle Arnaud Gallery, etc.